TIMMY O'DOWD AND THE BIG DITCH

TIMMY O'DOWD
AND THE BIG DITCH

A STORY
OF THE
GLORY
DAYS
ON THE
OLD
ERIE
CANAL
BY
LEN HILTS

GULLIVER BOOKS
HARCOURT BRACE & COMPANY
San Diego   New York   London

Requests for permission to make copies of any part of the work should be
mailed to: Permissions Department, Harcourt Brace & Company,
6277 Sea Harbor Drive, Orlando, Florida 32887-6777.

Library of Congress Cataloging-in-Publication Data
Hilts, Len.
Timmy O'Dowd and the big ditch.
"Gulliver Books."
Summary: In the late 1800s, young Timmy O'Dowd and his "city boy"
cousin must forget their differences and pool their energies when the Erie
Canal is damaged by storms.
1. Erie Canal (N.Y.) — Juvenile fiction. [1. Erie Canal
(N.Y.) — Fiction. 2. Cousins — Fiction] I. Title.
PZ7.H5678Ti   1988   [Fic]   88-16302
ISBN 0-15-200606-0

Printed in the United States of America
B C D E F

TO MARY SHURA CRAIG,
WARM FRIEND AND FINE WRITER, WHO WAS
TIMMY'S GODMOTHER.

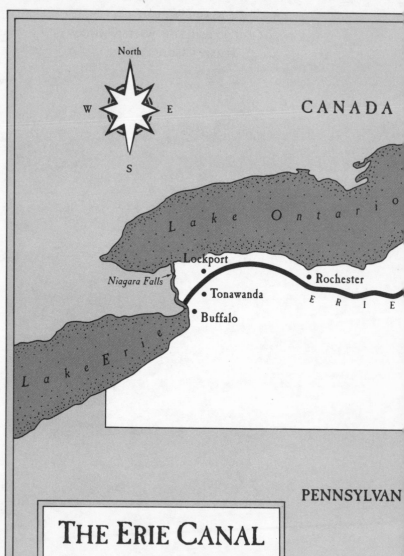

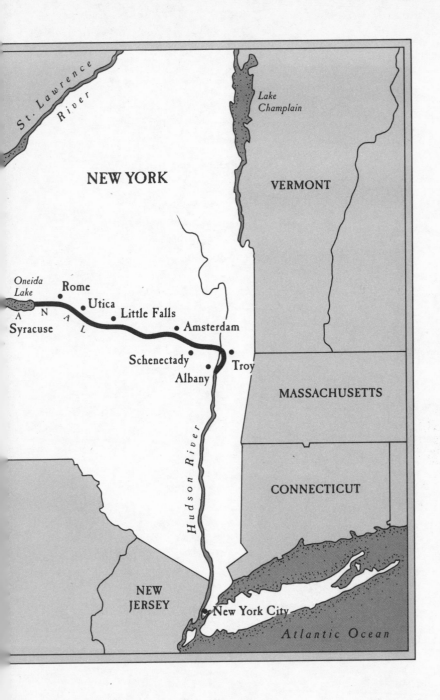

ABOUT THIS STORY

Timmy O'Dowd's family lived in western New York State, by the busy Erie Canal in 1845, when Timmy was twelve. Timmy's father, Patrick O'Dowd, was the superintendent of a section of the canal. Timmy's grandfather, who had helped build the canal twenty-five years earlier, had retired and now lived with the family. Timmy looked after the horses that towed one of the canal's emergency "hurry-up" boats.

Each day all summer long, dozens of freight barges and passenger packets moved past the O'Dowd's house on their way to Buffalo, at the western end, or Albany, at the eastern end of the canal.

Before the canal, New York State west of Albany was an untamed wilderness. A few rough trails connected its scattered pioneer farms and settlements. People along the Eastern Seaboard and thousands of immigrants from Europe itched to go to the new lands opening up in the West, but the terrible hardships of wilderness travel kept them home.

"The West" in those days was what is now Ohio, Michigan, Indiana, Illinois, Wisconsin, Iowa, and Minnesota. A family could get a 160-acre government grant in these unsettled lands if they cleared the land and built a homestead. Many people hoped in this way to make their dream of owning land come true.

Those pioneers who bravely moved west found an unexpected problem: It was too expensive and dangerous to ship the crops raised on their new farms to markets in New York and Boston. The only means of shipment were six-horse freight wagons, which could haul only three tons at a time over almost non-existent roads. A wagon took at least fifteen days to go from Buffalo to Albany, and the charge was a hundred dollars a ton.

The Erie Canal changed this. After its completion, it became the watery "Main Street" of the nation, connecting East Coast cities with the opening western lands.

Begun near Utica, New York, in 1817, the canal was in operation by October 1825.

After that, eighty-foot freight barges hauled fifty tons per trip from Lake Erie to the Hudson River in six to ten days. Shipping costs dropped to six dollars a ton, giving farmers a practical path to their markets.

Travelers no longer faced jolting trips by horse, wagon, or stage. From Albany to Buffalo on a passenger packet was a few days of easy travel. At Buffalo, lake ships waited to take them on to Detroit or Chicago.

Small wilderness villages, including Schenectady and Rochester, suddenly blossomed into major towns after the canal opened. Inns sprang up all along the route. New farms appeared beside it. A whole new breed of people, who called themselves the canawlers, operated the canal and the boats that worked on it.

Timmy O'Dowd and his family were canawlers, and this is the story of one summer in their lives.

TIMMY O'DOWD AND THE BIG DITCH

CHAPTER 1

When Timmy heard the brassy blare of Cap'n Sam's horn, he dropped his shovel and dashed from the stable to the wharf. Although the *Glory Be* was still a mile up the canal, he could see Cap'n Sam standing in all his splendor on her bridge, looking ten feet tall in his top hat. The bright blue of his frock coat matched the azure of the sky, and the horn at his lips glinted like a jewel in the sunlight.

Timmy's heart raced. Not another packet on the canal could hold a candle to the *Glory Be*. While Cap'n Sam strutted, passengers lounged on the forward deck and on top of the cabin, chatting and sipping cool drinks.

For a moment, Timmy saw himself standing by the tiller, master of all he could see—the proud *Glory Be*, the canal before him, the passengers, the horses. He felt wonderful.

Someday, someday . . .

Billy, the hoggee riding the second horse in the boat's two-horse hitch, moved the team smartly along the towpath. The strong gait of the matched black horses kept the towrope taut. When asked, they could haul the packet at eight miles an hour—even though that was well over the speed limit.

Timmy smiled. Cap'n Sam demanded a smart, fast-traveling pair for his boat every time he switched teams at his line's replacement stables.

Grandfather heard the horn, too, and hurried from the bunkhouse, limping to favor his game leg. He'd been playing checkers with the hurry-up crew. When he sat for a long time, his game leg took a while to warm up.

"Sounds like old Sam Blunt acomin'," he said. "No doubt he's speedin'. He allus does. Patrick ought to slap a fine on him."

"He's trying to break the Schenectady-to-Buffalo record," Timmy said.

"He's been tryin' for ten years," Grandfather scoffed. He squinted for a better look, then shook his head. "He's a sight, that old Blunt, dressed like a rooster struttin' on the hen-yard fence. Look at that! Yellow pantaloons, no less!"

Timmy grinned in open admiration. "Someday that'll be me. I'll have a packet like that and a tall beaver hat like Cap'n Sam's. But I think I'll wear a bright red coat."

Grandfather snorted. "Not while I'm alive, you won't! Red coats are a sad sight for any Irishman."

Timmy's mother joined them on the wharf.

"Timothy'll have himself a lovely emerald green coat, Michael. I'll see to it myself."

Her face was flushed from the heat of the kitchen. She untied her apron, threw it over her arm, and began poking strands of red hair into her bun. "I'm a sight," she said to no one in particular.

Grandfather chuckled. "You're a sight for these old eyes, Kate. I'll take you the way you are. If there's anythin' I like better'n you, it's your cookin'."

Kate blushed. "Away with you, Michael O'Dowd. I don't know which has more blarney in him, you or your

2

son. You're both scoundrels." She looked around. "Where's your father, Timmy?"

"Da and Mr. Connarty took the boat to fix a leak at Weber's place," Timmy said. "He won't be long."

The hooves of the tow team sounded like the beating of a bass drum as they trotted from the towpath onto O'Dowd's wooden wharf.

Billy, the hoggee, grinned down at Timmy. "Hello, Irish. Say, have we got a surprise fer you on the boat!"

As he spoke, Cap'n Sam bellowed, "Whoa them down, Billy! We're pullin' in here for a minute." He leaned on the tiller, and the bow of the packet thumped the wharf.

The passengers turned toward the captain to see why they were stopping.

"This here is O'Dowd's place," Cap'n Sam announced in his ringmaster voice. "We're lettin' off a passenger." He paused, then shouted at Timmy's mother, "Kate! You bakin' today?"

She nodded.

Cap'n Sam roared, "Any of you got a taste for pie? Kate O'Dowd's are the best in all New York State!"

Kate muttered to Timmy, "I didn't bake that many."

But it was too late. The passengers were stepping to the wharf and heading her way. She fled to the kitchen.

Timmy watched Ethan, Cap'n Sam's black cabin boy, haul a heavy carpetbag and a heavier flat canvas case over the side. Behind him, a boy emerged from the cabin and disembarked. Timmy's eyes popped.

The boy, about his own age, wore a tailored suit and a wide-brimmed straw hat garnished with a bright yellow ribbon. His fine white linen shirt, topped by a tall, stiff collar, sported ruffles and a soft flowing neckerchief. To finish it off, he wore white stockings and shiny black shoes.

A real macaroni!

The boy stood beside his luggage and took in the wharf, the cobblestone house, the porch, the stables, and the bunkhouse. His face screwed into a frown that said he didn't want to be here.

Grandfather, staring, too, said, "That boy-o is surely dressed for a weddin' or a funeral. Nobody here is dead or gettin' married, so why's he gettin' off?"

Cap'n Sam swaggered from the boat and approached them with an envelope in his hand.

"Got a letter for you, Mr. O'Dowd," he said as he handed it to Grandfather, "from your son Donal in New York." He jerked his head toward the wharf. "That's his boy."

"Saints be!" Grandfather said. "You mean that's little Dennis?" His surprise turned to concern. "Has somethin' happened to Donal?"

Cap'n Sam laughed. "Naw, he's fine. Talked to him myself when he brought the lad to the dock at Schenectady."

He lowered his voice to a conspiratorial whisper. "He thinks the boy's too citified. Wants him to spend two weeks with Timmy so he can get to know his cousin and the canal."

The picture came together for Timmy. This was Dennis O'Dowd, the son of Uncle Donal, who lived in New York City. Uncle Donal used to work on the canal, but he went to the city with only a wagon and a team of horses. Soon he had a dozen teams working for him, what with all the hauling business because of canal freight. Kate read his infrequent letters aloud to Grandfather.

"Your son's gettin' to be a rich man," Cap'n Sam said.

Grandfather eyed Dennis's fine clothes. "I can see that," he said.

4

Timmy sauntered over to Dennis. "I'm Timmy," he said. "We're cousins."

Dennis's eyes traveled from the top of Timmy's tattered straw hat to his dusty bare feet. His upper lip curled a little, and his nose twitched.

"Do you always dress like that?" he asked.

"'Cept when I go to church," Timmy replied. "This is how everybody dresses around here. We work."

Now Timmy slowly walked around Dennis, playing the same game. He inspected the suit, the clean white shirt, the yellow ribbon on his cousin's hat. In all his days, he had never seen anyone dressed like that on a weekday. On Sunday maybe, but never on a weekday.

Dennis followed him with his eyes.

Timmy's curiosity itched. He had never touched a soft, smooth fabric like that of Dennis's jacket. He reached out to it.

Dennis jumped away. "Don't do that! It's velvet, and you'll get it dirty."

Timmy rammed his hands into his pants pockets.

"Well, you're a regular *dandy*, aren't you? Cap'n Sam says you're goin' to stay two weeks. You figure to dress like that the whole time?"

Timmy chuckled as he pictured Dennis in his fancy clothes shoveling out the stable. Caring for the horses that pulled the hurry-up boat was one of Timmy's jobs. He had to see that the horses were fit to run hard when a canal wall breached, which meant hauling hay and water and shoveling a lot of manure. The crew had to reach the breaks quickly, before the water flooded the crops on nearby farms.

He said, "You goin' to work while you're here? A little manure might help the look of that velvet."

"I'm going to sketch," Dennis said defiantly.

5

"Sketch?" Timmy said. "What's that?"

"It means to draw."

"You goin' to draw pictures? I used to draw pictures when I was little. Not any more, though. Now I work."

Dennis had had enough of this conversation. He headed back toward the boat and said to Cap'n Sam, "I want to get back aboard. I'm not staying here."

Cap'n Sam had raised his horn, which hung on a gold chain around his neck, to his lips. He blew a long, resonant note, then announced in a booming voice, "All aboard now! The *Glory Be* is shovin' off!"

The passengers, standing around a table on the porch, finished off their slices of succulent peach pie. Kate was giving them damp cloths to wipe the sweet juice from their fingers before they hurried back to the boat.

Timmy watched Michael O'Dowd approach the newcomer. "Dennis," he said, "I'm your grandfather. Shake hands."

Dennis took the old man's hand respectfully. "Good afternoon, sir."

Grandfather said, "Well, now, it's a fine thing to have you visitin' me for a while. We'll have some talks, you and me and Timmy."

Dennis looked sheepish. "I'm sorry, Grandfather, but I'm not staying," he said. "I can't stay."

"No?" Grandfather said. "And why would that be?"

"Well," Dennis said uncertainly, "I don't think I have the right clothes."

"Aw now, Dennis." Grandfather laughed. "Do you think we've got no extra clothes at all around here? Sure, just as soon as you take off that fine suit, Timmy'll give you some sturdy workin' clothes. You'll have no problems."

Cap'n Sam gave another blast on the horn and reached

6

out to shake Grandfather's hand. "I'll pick the boy up in two weeks, Mr. O'Dowd," he said.

"But I'm not staying!" Dennis protested.

Grandfather put his arm around Dennis and steered him toward his baggage.

"Now just get your bags there, Dennis, and we'll go inside. I'll introduce you to the leprechaun that lives with us. Timmy'll show you the stables and the horses. Come along now, boy."

"Leprechaun?" Dennis looked up at his grand-father, startled. "He lives with you?"

"Grandfather!" Timmy protested, "Don't tell him that. No leprechaun lives with us."

"Well," said Grandfather with twinkling eyes, "he doesn't exactly *live* with us. But he's around all the time just the same, makin' one mischief after another. I don't doubt he's over there in the weeds right now, watchin' us every minute."

Kate came from the kitchen. "If that fool leprechaun is watching us," she said sharply, "why don't you have him carry the boy's bags, Michael?"

She turned, all smiles, to Dennis. "Welcome to our house, Dennis O'Dowd. It's glad I am to have you here. And how are your father and mother? We haven't seen them in a month of Sundays."

Timmy's insides curdled. His mother was trying to make the little stuffed shirt feel welcome. He shook his head. This was going to be a long two weeks.

Dennis picked up his bag. Kate said, "Timmy, give him a hand."

Timmy had to use both hands to swing the canvas case up to his shoulders. *It must be loaded with rocks*, he thought. *What in the world can the little dandy have in it?*

7

Struggling under the weight, he followed his mother and his cousin to the house. His eyes fell on Dennis's jacket. He felt a strong urge to wipe his sweaty palms on the beautiful fabric.

Grandfather chuckled softly. "Your face looks like a prune."

"Am I *really* goin' to have him around for weeks, Daideo?" Timmy asked desperately.

Grandfather's hand was warm on his shoulder. "Let me lean on you, boy-o, while we walk. Me leg is achin' a bit."

They started up the path. "Timmy," the old man's voice came soft, "Dennis is an O'Dowd, one of us. He's got to have a lot of good in him, even if it's hard to see under them clothes. But when he tastes life here on the canal, the good will come out. See if it don't."

Cap'n Sam gave one final blast on his horn as the boat moved out into the canal. Then he shouted, "Timmy, I nearly forgot. You goin' to be my apprentice on the *Glory Be* next summer?"

The misery inside Timmy skyrocketed into elation. He spun around so fast he almost knocked Grandfather down.

"You bet, Cap'n Sam! You bet I will!"

Billy flicked his whip over the horses, and the *Glory Be* pulled away toward Buffalo.

Grandfather looked after the boat and shook his head. "Does your father know about this?" he asked.

CHAPTER 2

Kate and Dennis were already inside. Timmy followed, blinking in the subdued light after the bright sun. He dropped the canvas case with a loud thud and said, "Here are your rocks."

"Those are my books," his cousin told him. "You don't have to wreck them, do you?"

"Books!" Timmy blurted. "Jehoshaphat! What for?"

Dennis shrugged and turned back to Kate. She was in the middle of the big room, saying, "This is where we do most of our living in this house, Dennis, the keeping room."

Dennis put his bag down and surveyed the room. A stone fireplace half filled one wall. To the right of the fireplace was a wooden sink and a black wood-burning stove. A big table with a dozen chairs stood a short distance from the stove.

"That side's my kitchen, " she said. "We eat at the table."

"It's a big table for just four people."

"Oh, there's more than four of us," Kate said. "Did you see the bunkhouse next door? The six men of the hurry-up crew sleep there and eat with us in here."

She pointed to the other side of the room, where chairs were arranged in a comfortable semicircle. "That's our sitting room," she said.

She indicated two doorways in the back wall, hung with bright flowered curtains. "That room is Grandfather's and the other is where Mr. O'Dowd and I sleep."

"Where's Timmy's room?"

Kate pointed to a ladder. "Up in the loft. There's plenty of room up there for both of you."

Exasperation clawed at Timmy. There it was already! Dennis was to wear his clothes, sleep in his loft. Well, the dandy could carry his own heavy baggage up the ladder.

Kate said, "Timmy will stuff a straw ticking for you."

Timmy thought, *no dumb city dandy would know how to do that, so I have to do it for him.* He started to protest, but Grandfather's fingers squeezed his shoulder in warning. His voice was low. "Dennis is our guest."

When loud voices sounded outside, Timmy shouted, "Da's back," and ran out to the wharf.

Patrick O'Dowd was watching the hurry-up crew run the boat into its slip, cut into the canal wall. With the boat in, he dropped the wooden wharf extension in place.

"Kate, we're home," he shouted. "When's supper?"

Kate appeared on the porch with Dennis at her side.

O'Dowd turned to Timmy, "Who's that?"

Timmy made a face. "Cousin Dennis from New York City."

"Donal's boy?" O'Dowd's face brightened with delight. "Is Donal here, too?"

"Just him," Timmy said, jerking his thumb in the direction of the house.

O'Dowd darted an amused look at his son.

"Don't like him much, do you?"

Timmy stared at the ground and shook his head.

"What'd he do to you?"

Timmy couldn't explain why he didn't like Dennis. The boy hadn't done anything. It was just—well—that he was there. But that wouldn't make any sense to his father.

"Aw, I guess it's his clothes and all," he said finally.

O'Dowd welcomed Dennis with a cheery, "'Pon my soul, lad, you're the very image of your father. How is Donal—and your mother?"

Dennis flushed and shook hands. "Just fine, sir. They said to give you their best."

Kate murmured, "What nice manners!"

Timmy glowered. Nobody ever said *his* manners were nice. They just told him to mind them.

"Kate," O'Dowd said, "if we've a few minutes before supper, I'll show Dennis the hurry-up boat."

"Ten minutes," Kate told him and went inside.

"Come on, Dennis." O'Dowd put his arm around the velvet jacket. "I'll bet you've never seen a hurry-up boat in the city."

The two started toward the wharf. Timmy trotted after them, frowning.

On the deck of the hurry-up boat, O'Dowd told Dennis, "When the canal was dug, the dirt from the channel was piled up to make the walls on either side."

From where Dennis stood, the canal looked like two long earthen embankments with water between them.

"How deep is the water?" he asked.

"Four feet," his uncle replied. "But now they've started makin' it deeper so bigger boats can use the canal. It's forty feet wide at the top and twenty-eight feet at the bottom. The sides are tapered."

Dennis leaned over the water to study the tapering

11

walls. "The captain of the *Glory Be* told us how the walls sometimes break. They look pretty solid to me."

"Oh, that they are," O'Dowd said, "except when they're abused. High waves from speedin' canal boats lap at them. And when heavy rains overfill the canal, the walls get soft and mushy."

"Why didn't they make the walls of stone?" asked Dennis. "The locks are stone. Why not the walls?"

"Good question," O'Dowd said. "The canawlers built locks and aqueducts of stone, but stone construction was too slow and costly for the whole 363 miles. You see, a lot of New Yorkers thought the canal was a bad idea. They called it Clinton's Ditch, and grumbled at every dollar Governor Clinton spent. So Clinton and the canawlers tried to finish the Erie as soon as possible, to prove what a grand idea it was."

"How long did it take?"

"Seven years," O'Dowd told him.

"Did everyone like the canal after that?"

"Most everyone. And why not? The canal makes money for the state, and it's turned New York City into the country's biggest port.

"The most amazin' thing," he continued, "is that the first canawlers didn't know anything about canal buildin'. They were mostly farmers, but they used their native good sense, made the walls of dirt, and got the job done.

"Critics were bettin' the dirt banks wouldn't hold the water. The day they let water into the canal, most everyone held his breath, just waitin' for the walls to collapse. But they worked fine. The canawlers had fooled 'em by linin' the walls with clay."

"But they do break open," Dennis reminded him.

"True, and we have to watch 'em careful-like. But with

12

the canal makin' money, we're rebuildin' it a bit at a time. It's goin' to be wider and deeper, and it's goin' to have stone walls. Meanwhile, we've got to make those dirt banks hold."

He turned back to the hurry-up boat. "Anyway, when the walls break open, the water pours onto farms next to the canal—and all tarnation busts loose. You've never seen anyone madder than a farmer when his land is flooded. Believe me, we pay dearly in damages."

"How many hurry-up boats are there?" Dennis asked.

"Oh, one every thirty miles or so along the canal. We run like rabbits to fix breaks before too much water gets out."

He laughed. "I tell you, Dennis, next to a wet farmer, the maddest man in the world is a barge captain whose boat is grounded because the water level has dropped."

Dennis's eyes traveled over the materials and equipment neatly stacked on the deck.

"Do you use all of this?" he asked.

"We keep most everything we need to fix a bad break." He pointed to a pile of boards. "Like those planks. We ram them into breaches in the berm. They stop the water flow while we patch the hole."

"Berm?"

"Oh, that's what canawlers call the canal walls: berms. The towpath is on the top of the berm on this side."

They walked forward on the boat.

"We use that hay," he said, indicating golden bales of hay in the bow, "for smaller breaks. We make patches with mud, sticks, and hay."

Neat coils of rope lay near the cabin. Inside, dozens of tools—spades, picks, shovels, pry bars, axes, and big wooden mallets—hung on racks. A row of lanterns stood on a shelf near the window. "We can even work at night if we have to," O'Dowd said.

Timmy, perched on a rope coil, watched his father's performance. *You'd think he was showin' the boat to President Polk himself*, he thought. *Maybe we ought to have a brass band.*

The noisy clatter of an old cowbell shattered the late-afternoon quiet. Grandfather, swinging the bell on the porch, shouted, "Supper's ready!"

Timmy jumped down, relieved that the hurry-up boat tour was over.

"Come on, Da. Time to eat."

Dennis's place at the table was between Timmy and Grandfather. He stood behind his chair while the others noisily pulled out theirs and settled at the table. The leathery-faced men of the crew sat around the lower end of the table.

Grandfather said, "Aren't you goin' to sit, Dennis?"

The boy glanced at Kate, who was carrying serving dishes from the big wood stove to the table. She smiled broadly. "It's all right, Dennis. Don't wait for me. I thank you for the courtesy, but we don't stand on ceremony here."

Dennis sat down, and his uncle said grace.

Timmy's appetite was sharp and ready. Dinner, their big meal, was at noon, but by suppertime Timmy was always hungry again.

Tonight they had one of his favorites—sliced beef to lay on Kate's brown-crusted bread and drown with her good brown gravy.

The clinking of knives and forks was the only sound in the room as everyone got down to business. When Dennis took only a small helping of beef and one piece of bread, Timmy nudged him.

"Better take all you want right now," he advised.

Grandfather laughed. "He's right, Dennis. If a platter gets past you, it may never come back." He nodded at the crewmen. "Those vultures eat like every meal was their last."

Sean Connarty, the crew chief, who was nearly as old as Grandfather, guffawed. "Don't let the old man tease you, boy. Nobody ever left Kate O'Dowd's table hungry."

Grandfather turned to Dennis. "Eatin' is pretty important to us, Dennis. When we were lads in Ireland, we were lucky to get a few potatoes for supper."

Connarty nodded. "When we came to America, things were so bad we didn't even have *potatoes*. It's even worse over there now."

Dennis looked at his grandfather. "My father said you came from Ireland to work on the canal."

"Aye," Grandfather said. "'Twas in 1817. You see, the canal people sent Mr. Canvass White to England to study the canals there. Before he came back, he hired a famous Irish canal man, J. J. McShane, to come over here to help. Old McShane told him he needed some strong Irish backs to get the job done. So we were hired."

"Aye," Connarty said. "Strong backs and weak minds!"

"Now, Sean, the work was hard, but you know it was lovely to have it—and the good things we got from it."

"Good things and bad," Connarty agreed. "Don't forget the mosquitoes big as horses, the cholera and swamp fever. Do you mind the time we worked the Montezuma Swamp, near Rochester, Michael? It's a wonder we ever finished that part, with every man down sick most of the time."

15

"We never would have, except by workin' in the winter," Grandfather replied, "when the skeeters took their holiday."

After everyone had eaten, Kate brought in the peach pie.

"Only one piece each tonight," she said sternly. "That fool Blunt sold all the rest to his passengers. He's always doing that. I wish he'd warn me in advance."

"Now, Kate," her husband said, laughing, "you know you like the extra money. How else could you buy the material for pretty dresses like the one you're wearin'?"

Kate shook her head. "That won't work, Patrick O'Dowd. Your blarney gets you only one piece of pie, like everyone else."

The crewmen laughed.

While waiting for his pie, Grandfather pushed back his chair and walked to the door. He peered out for a moment, then returned.

"The leprechaun has his umbrella out," he announced.

The crew burst into laughter, and Connarty turned to Dennis. "That means the old man's corns are hurtin' and it's goin' to rain. He allus blames it on the leprechaun."

"My corns *are* achin' somewhat," Grandfather admitted. "But when that little green fella gets his bumbershoot out, you can wager it's goin' to be a bad un. He don't like to get wet."

Connarty pushed back from the table. "Well, boys, it's bed for us. We could be up and runnin' afore mornin'."

CHAPTER 3

After the hurry-up crew left for the bunkhouse, the O'Dowds settled in the sitting area. O'Dowd smiled at Dennis. "I suspect you have a regular parlor, Dennis. This is ours."

Dennis nodded. "A front and a back parlor. I'm not supposed to go into the front parlor except on Sunday or when we have company."

Timmy frowned. Two parlors? They really spread it on thick, didn't they?

"Well," his father went on, "here on the canal we make this one big room do it all—kitchen, parlor, everything."

O'Dowd sat in his cushioned chair with a little table beside it that held his pipe and a tobacco canister. Grandfather's rocking chair was on the other side of the table, so he, too, could reach the pipe tobacco. Timmy took his usual place on the floor in front of them.

Dennis stayed behind to help Kate clear the supper dishes.

"Why, thank you, Dennis," Kate said. She glared at Timmy. "It's nice to have a helping hand."

Timmy jumped to his feet and headed for the table.

"It's my job at home," Dennis explained.

"I clean the stables and do the garden and the stove wood," Timmy said pointedly.

"So you do," Kate interrupted, "and the work hasn't killed you yet."

Timmy clamped his mouth shut. That was another black mark against Dennis in the score book of his mind. This little macaroni had a few things coming to him. "Wait till I get him in the stables," Timmy promised himself.

Dishes done, Kate and the boys joined the men. Kate pulled a sewing box closer to her chair and turned up the oil lamp beside her.

"Well, now, Dennis," Timmy's father said. "I suppose you go to school in the city?"

"Yes, sir," Dennis replied. "I go to regular school and to art school."

"Art school? Well!"

"I'm going to be an artist."

Timmy had been waiting for an opportunity like this. "What good's an artist?" he asked. "Girls draw pictures. Men work."

Grandfather said, "Whoa there, Timmy. If the lad wants to be an artist, why shouldn't he?"

"Why in tarnation would anyone want to be one anyway?" Timmy was scornful.

"I want to," Dennis replied. "That's reason enough. My father says a man should be what he wants to be." He looked at Timmy. "What are *you* going to be?"

An uneasy silence fell over the room. Timmy glanced at his grandfather, who warned him by shaking his head slightly.

Before Timmy could answer, his father said, "He's goin' to be a canal engineer. Now there's a future! Look at all the canals bein' built. And livin' and workin' on the canal as he has, Timmy has a fine start."

Timmy wriggled uncomfortably.

"We're savin' for his schoolin'," his father went on. "He'll go to Rensselaer Tech, over at Troy, when he's ready. I've already talked to the schoolmaster about it."

"Are you a canal engineer, Uncle Patrick?" Dennis asked.

"No, Dennis, I'm just a section superintendent."

"You're as good as an engineer, Patrick," Kate said. "You have to be to do what you do."

"You might say I'm a self-trained engineer," he conceded. "But that's not good enough any more. Now, engineers need to be schooled. That's why Timmy is goin' to Rensselaer, where they teach canal engineering."

Another strained silence fell. Everyone was looking at Timmy.

Kate spoke up quickly. "I hope you brought some of your art with you, Dennis."

"I drew some on the boat," he said. "Would you like to see what I did?"

"Oh, yes," Kate replied.

Timmy watched as Dennis climbed the ladder to the loft. His mother was as bad as his father, putting on all these company manners for this little dandy.

Dennis returned with a small sheaf of papers. He shuffled through them and handed one to Kate. Timmy rose and stood behind her, looking past her shoulder. The drawing was of a canal boat passing under a low bridge.

"Why, that's the *Glory Be!*" Kate exclaimed. "I'd know it anywhere." She looked more closely at the drawing. "My, Dennis, this is very good. Look here, Timmy."

Timmy was looking. It was as if he were standing behind Cap'n Sam, looking toward the *Glory Be*'s bow. The packet was passing under a bridge. A farmer on the bridge waved to the passengers. Two men atop the deckhouse lay flat on their bellies. The bridge would miss them by only a foot or so if they kept their heads down.

"Say, that *is* pretty good," Timmy said grudgingly. "You really draw it?"

Dennis nodded. "I drew a lot on the boat." He pulled another paper from the stack.

Timmy stared even harder at this drawing. There was Cap'n Sam, standing straight and important near the tiller. Even though the sketch was in pencil, black lines on white paper, Timmy could *see* the color of the captain's blue coat, yellow pantaloons, and shiny black boots. Cap'n Sam was blowing his horn, and its blare filled Timmy's imagination.

"It looks real!" he said, not even trying to hide his admiration.

O'Dowd and Grandfather now stood behind Kate, too, watching as Dennis brought out another sheet.

"I brought this one from home," he said, handing it to Kate. "I thought you might like it for your wall."

The drawing pictured a rakish three-masted clipper ship dressed in full sail. White spindrift curled back from her bow, and her canvas billowed before the wind.

"At the New York docks you can see ships from all over the world. This is an American clipper, bound for California. I saw it heading out of New York harbor, to go round Cape Horn."

"Oh, I'd be proud to hang that on our wall," Kate said. "Right about there, I think." She pointed to a spot near the front window.

Grandfather squinted through his spectacles. "I could make a nice oak frame for that." He looked at his son. "Course, you'd have to buy a bit o' glass for it, Patrick. Would you want to do that?"

O'Dowd held the drawing up. "Of course I would. This is fine work, Dennis, and we're honored to have it."

"Clippers are the fastest ships in the world," Dennis said.

"Faster than a packet?" Timmy asked. "Packets can go eight miles an hour, or better."

"They better not, not while I'm around," said his father.

"Faster than that," Dennis replied. "When I go to Paris to study art, I'm going on a clipper. Of course, that'll be a couple of years yet, but I'm going."

The conversation settled down to talk about Dennis's family in New York. Soon, Grandfather began to nod.

O'Dowd tapped his shoulder. "Time for bed, Da," he said gently.

Grandfather, startled, sat up straight. "I was restin' me eyes, Patrick," he said.

"I know," Timmy's father replied. "But it's off to bed for all of us. Tomorrow comes early."

"I'd like to make some sketches while I'm here," Dennis said. "I'd like to do Grandfather and . . ."

"Tell you what," O'Dowd said. "You help Timmy with his chores in the mornin'. Then you can draw for the whole rest of the day if you want."

He looked hard at Timmy. "You two are goin' to be good friends."

In the loft, Timmy undressed silently and crawled under the bright quilt his mother had made for him. Dennis tested the softness of the straw mattress before lying down on it.

After a while, Dennis said, "You really going to be a canal engineer?"

Timmy hesitated before answering; then his tone was defiant. "I'm goin' to be a packet-boat captain, like Cap'n Sam."

"I thought so," Dennis said. "I knew something was wrong when your father talked about your going to college."

Timmy sat up, his eyes glowing. "I'm goin' to have a fine tall hat and a green coat and I'm goin' to break the record from Schenectady to Buffalo. My boat's goin' to be the *Flying Eagle*."

"How do you get to be a captain?" Dennis asked. "Is there a school for it?"

"Not a regular school," Timmy told him. "Cap'n Sam's goin' to 'prentice me on his packet next summer, and I'm goin' to learn. Course, I already know a lot."

He stood up and swaggered across the room. "Whip 'em up, Billy!" he boomed. "We ain't waitin' for the freighters, you know." He pretended to bring a horn to his lips and give a mighty blast. "'Hoy there, the lock! Packet comin' through!"

"That's Cap'n Sam." Dennis laughed. "Can't be anyone else."

Timmy suddenly ducked down. "Low bridge! Everybody down!" he bellowed. "Low bridge! Low bridge! Mind your heads."

Kate's voice called from below, "You boys settle down, you hear!"

"Yes, ma'am," Dennis said, and giggled. Then he whispered, "Those bridges are terrible. The first one almost killed me. You have to fall on your face every few minutes. Why did they build so many low bridges?"

"Grandfather says the farmers wouldn't let 'em dig the canal through their land unless each one got a bridge. They promised so many that they built 'em low to save money."

"What about your father? Will he let you go with Cap'n Sam?"

Timmy's elation disappeared. He collapsed onto his bed. "I don't know," he said miserably. "I just don't know. I only know I'm goin' to be a packet captain. That's all I've ever wanted to be in my whole life."

Dennis said nothing for a moment, and Timmy went on. "You're lucky your father doesn't stand in your way."

"Oh, but he does," Dennis replied.

"You said you were goin' to Paris to study art," Timmy reminded him.

"That's what I *want* to do," Dennis replied. "He *wants* me to go into his business."

"I thought your father said a man ought to be what he wants to be," Timmy said, thoroughly confused.

Dennis sighed. "He did. But he thinks I ought to *want* to be in his business."

O'Dowd's voice boomed from below. "All right, you two! Those stables will be waitin' in the mornin'!"

The boys exchanged glances, and Timmy blew out the candle. Dennis said, "Good night, Timmy."

Timmy closed his eyes and mumbled, "G'night." He was feeling mixed up. Maybe Dennis wasn't so bad after all. But two parlors, a ton of books, and a velvet coat! He sighed. It was hard to know what to think.

CHAPTER 4

Timmy rummaged in the pine chest where he kept his clothes and found a pair of pants and a flannel shirt. "Put these on," he told Dennis. "We've got work to do."

He handed him a pair of work shoes. "I mostly don't wear shoes in the summer," he said, "'cept when I clean the stable."

Dennis tightened a worn leather belt around his waist and hiked up the shapeless baggy pants. The flannel shirt was an indefinable color, mostly brown and red. The sleeves were too long, so he rolled them up.

"These don't look very good," he said.

"The horses don't care," Timmy replied.

Kate had steaming bowls of porridge topped with lumps of golden butter waiting when they came down the ladder. Timmy sprinkled brown sugar on his, then flooded it with rich milk. Dennis watched and did the same.

"You ever groom a horse?" Timmy asked between spoonfuls.

"Tom, the stableboy, does that."

"I'm the stableboy here," Timmy said sourly. There it was again! Dennis really puts on airs, he thought. Dennis caught the change in Timmy's voice. "I'm sorry. I didn't mean . . ."

"What *can* you do?" Timmy cut in. "Not much, I guess, 'cept draw." He remembered the heavy canvas case and added, "And read books."

Dennis looked Timmy straight in the eye. "I can hitch a team."

"Well, that's somethin'," Timmy said, backing down. "Course, we only hitch 'em up when the hurry-up crew goes out. But they have to be good and ready for that."

He licked the last of the porridge from his spoon and stood up. "Come on."

"Don't forget the apples," Kate said.

Timmy took four apples from a bowl in the center of the table, put one in each pocket of his pants, and gave two to Dennis. "Put these in your pockets," he said.

Dennis did as he was told. "They're lumpy," he complained. Timmy waved him out the door.

The big brown horse in the end stall neighed and stomped his white-stockinged forefoot when he heard Timmy coming.

"This is Mayo," Timmy told Dennis. "He and Galway"—he nodded at the horse in the next stall—"are a matched pair. They can make that hurry-up boat fly. The mares at the other end are Shannon and Tralee. Tralee is sort of my horse. Da usually rides Shannon."

"They're named after places in Ireland," Dennis noted.

"Grandfather named them. He wants to remember places he's been."

Timmy fondled Mayo's soft nose. The horse nickered

and poked inquisitively into his shirt. "He's lookin' for his apple. I bring him one every day."

Timmy pulled an apple from his deep pocket and offered it to the horse on his open palm. Mayo's big head swung up. He took the apple gently and began crunching with great satisfaction.

Galway caught the sweet apple smell, tossed his head, and snorted, as if saying, "Where's mine?"

Timmy brought out the other apple, and Galway nibbled at his fingers. Timmy teased him by holding the apple tightly. The horse snuffled and snorted, his whiskers tickling Timmy's hand as he tried to take the fruit. The horse was gentle, but insistent. Timmy finally let the apple go. Galway tossed his head back and began chewing.

The mares waited patiently in the other stalls. They knew their turn was coming.

"They all like you," Dennis said.

"It's 'cause I like 'em. Horses know when you like 'em and when you don't. Do you like horses?"

"I don't rightly know," Dennis said. "Never had much to do with them except to ride."

"Well," Timmy said, "the main thing is to let 'em know you like 'em. Stroke 'em and talk soft and let 'em feel your hands on their skin. When you're near, move slow. Quick movements startle 'em."

He pointed to the mares. "Give your apples to Tralee and Shannon. Pet 'em and talk a little first."

As Dennis approached, holding out an apple, both mares stepped back. Their eyes asked, "Who is this?" Clearly they wanted their apples, but worried about getting them from a stranger.

Timmy watched from the far end of the stable. "You got to make friends with 'em," he said. "Move in slow-like. Reach out and touch their noses."

26

Dennis was clumsy and afraid, and the mares sensed it.

"Talk soft to 'em," Timmy said.

Dennis tried but just didn't have the knack. Ten minutes passed before Tralee came close enough to take her apple. Timmy had to come over to give the apple to Shannon.

"They think you're afraid," Timmy said.

"Not exactly afraid," Dennis said. "I'm just not accustomed to such big animals."

"You better get used to 'em," Timmy said. "Even artists need horses if they're goin' to get wherever they're goin'."

Timmy handed Dennis a shovel. "First, the manure goes onto that pile out back of the stable. Then we pull the old straw out of the stalls."

Mayo had finished his apple, decided it wasn't enough, and nuzzled Timmy for more hidden fruit. Timmy pushed his big nose away.

"We bring in new straw for the stalls," Timmy continued. "We put hay in the mangers and give each horse his ration of grain—one measure of oats." He pointed to empty buckets hanging near the door. "And we haul water for 'em from the well in those. The last thing we do is brush 'em down."

Dennis's nose twitched. "It smells in here."

"It's a stable," Timmy replied. "You know what a stable smells like. Your father has horses."

"Yes, but I don't like it."

"Start shovelin'," Timmy said in disgust. Dennis grasped the handle of the shovel as if it were a broom.

"Crimanettles!" Timmy said. "Don't you know nothin' at all? Here! Hold it like this!"

Timmy placed Dennis's hands correctly on the handle,

and Dennis lifted the shovel and went to work. He was clumsy and slow. By the time he had carried out his second shovelful, Timmy had cleaned the other three stalls.

Timmy leaned on his shovel.

"You're an artist, all right. You sure ain't much good at anything else."

Dennis straightened up and stood very still, staring at Timmy. His eyes flashed with fury. Then he hurled his shovel across the stable.

"I've taken all I'm going to take from you," he shouted. "All you've done since I got here is carp and criticize." Without warning, he lunged at Timmy.

Timmy jumped back, but was too slow. Dennis's flying body hit him hard and knocked him down. He rolled over instantly and scrambled to his feet, his fists cocked and ready. Dennis flew at him again, and the two clinched. Dennis's strength and anger startled Timmy. The sissy could fight.

They crashed to the floor again, rolling over and over, each trying to get on top. Timmy couldn't keep Dennis down, even for a second. He finally worked a fist free and landed a glancing blow on Dennis's cheek. Dennis drove his knee into Timmy's stomach. They careened into a rack of shovels, and the tools fell around them, clanging like crazy bells.

Timmy managed to get on top and sat astride Dennis. He aimed a punch at his cousin, but Dennis turned his head to avoid the blow, heaving his body in an attempt to throw Timmy off.

At that moment, Grandfather rushed into the stable, forgetting his game leg in his haste to see what the noise was all about. He grabbed Timmy by the shirt collar and jerked him off his cousin. He still had the strength of a digger in his arms.

"Now what kind o' nonsense is this?" he demanded.

Once Timmy was up, Dennis squirmed out of the way and got up on his feet. The boys, breathing like spent race horses, glared at each other.

"All right, who started this and what's it about?"

Neither boy replied.

Grandfather released Timmy. "Now, lads," he said in a calmer voice, "boys will be boys, and a little fight once in a while is a good thing."

He smiled broadly. "I was a fair brawler meself in the old days. But it don't do around here, between cousins."

The two boys continued to glare at each other.

"Kate'll have both of your scalps," Grandfather warned. "She don't tolerate fightin'."

Timmy remembered an afternoon the summer before, when he and Cap'n Sam's hoggee had squared off. Kate's anger had lasted two weeks. She had kept him chopping firewood morning, noon, and evening.

"If you have so much extra energy," she told him, "we'll put it to good use. Fight with that wood for a while."

Before Kate had cooled off, Timmy had chopped enough stove wood for the winter.

"All right," Grandfather said, "the fight's over. Shake hands."

The boys looked at him in disbelief.

"I told you to shake hands."

Neither Dennis nor Timmy moved. Grandfather waited. The horses watched, and Tralee whinnied.

Reluctantly, Dennis stuck out his hand. Timmy looked at it, then at Grandfather, who stared back at him, waiting. At last, Timmy took the offered hand. The two shook once, then dropped their hands.

Grandfather nodded. "That's a little better, but not much. We are goin' to stand here until the two of you shake hands like gentlemen. No fight is a good fight unless the fighters shake properly afterward."

The fighters stuck out their hands and executed a handshake that satisfied Grandfather.

"Ah, that's fine," the old man said. "Done like a pair of champions." He looked around the stable. "You get your work done in here?"

Timmy shook his head.

Grandfather said, "Get on with it then," and limped out of the stable.

CHAPTER 5

At noon, Timmy and Dennis sat beside each other at the table without speaking. Later, Timmy went to Kate's kitchen garden to take care of his weeding chores.

"Pull a dozen nice big carrots for supper," Kate told him. "Mind that the tops are sticking up before you pull."

The kitchen garden was a neat rectangle just beyond the barn. Orderly patches of carrots, spinach, cabbage, corn, and cucumbers grew side by side, making a pattern like a green patchwork quilt.

Beside it was his mother's special herb garden, providing the flavors that made her cooking so good. Timmy picked sage, dill, tarragon, basil, and thyme when Kate asked for them. In the early fall, she dried the herb leaves for use during the winter months.

In a small orchard beyond the garden, ripening yellow fruit hung like bright ornaments on two peach trees. Apple trees sagged from the weight of green apples, already tinged with red, that would be ready for picking in a month or so. Back of the orchard, a field of hay was nearly ready for mowing.

As Timmy looked at the maturing hay, he thought, I

hope the dandy is still here when hayin' comes. Then he'll find out what work is.

As he ran the hoe among heads of cabbage to clean out the weeds, he looked toward the house for signs of his cousin. He spotted Dennis on the porch, a board on his lap. He was bent over it, drawing, and his pencil moved rapidly over the paper.

"If he's not careful," Timmy said to himself, "he'll get calluses from all that sittin'. Wouldn't that be too bad?"

A bright sun tipped wavelets on the canal with sparkling crests as Dennis watched the never-ending stream of packets and freighters passing O'Dowd's. Horns, now close, now distant, sounded up and down the canal as the boats passed one another. Voices echoed over the water. The plink of a banjo rose over the voices as one boat passed.

On the western horizon, a pile of clouds was building into a gray cotton wall. Dennis saw faces form in the clouds, change, and disappear, to be replaced by more faces.

Grandfather came out and sat in the chair next to him. "You makin' pictures?"

Dennis shook his head. "Just practice sketches. You can see a long distance each way here, can't you."

"They call this the long level," Grandfather told him. "We've got sixty-nine miles that're flat and straight, without a lock 'til you get near Rochester."

He waved toward the west. "Afore you go back, Patrick'll show you Lockport. It's a grand sight. Five double locks, back to back, lift a barge more than sixty feet."

"Why sixty feet, Grandfather?"

"Well, you know 'bout Niagara Falls—that's the Niagara River tumblin' down a rock face. That same rock face runs 'cross this part of the state, and the locks at Lockport carry barges up and down it. Once a boat gets to the top at Lockport, it's a quick run to the end of the canal at Lake Erie."

Dennis had asked Cap'n Sam why a canal had locks.

"The canal is like a path with steps," the captain had answered. "Lake Erie is better'n five hundred feet higher than the Hudson River. Goin' west, like we are now, the *Glory Be* climbs the steps to Lake Erie. Comin' back east, she goes down the steps."

"How many lock steps are there?" Dennis had wanted to know.

"Eighty-three," Cap'n Sam replied, "if you count the ones you didn't see 'tween Schenectady and the river." He laughed, "If there weren't locks, all the water'd run out of Lake Erie and down into the Hudson River in a day. Wouldn't that be somethin'?"

Dennis continued to watch the busy boat traffic. Most of the boats were slow freighters. He saw barges with newly sawn lumber stacked on their decks. A small boat pushed a raft of logs fresh from a forest through the canal toward a lumbermill.

Grandfather told him, "The grain barges'll be comin' through after the corn harvest starts out in Michigan and Illinois."

"What does it cost to carry freight on the canal?" Dennis asked.

"Freighters pay accordin' to weight and the kind of load they're carryin'," Grandfather said. "Barges that carry salt travel free, 'cause everybody needs salt. Passenger packets pay six cents a mile."

"The locks get crowded," Dennis said, remembering

his trip from the city. Dozens of boats had lined up at each lock, waiting their turn to go through. The lockmaster could put only one through at a time, so a long line of boats formed on both sides of the lock.

Cap'n Sam had growled and stormed at every lock. He hated waiting. He was always trying to break the record for the run from Schenectady to Buffalo.

Every sixth or seventh boat passing O'Dowd's was a sleek passenger packet, each gaudier and more decorated than the last. Most were crowded with passengers.

Dennis had boarded the *Glory Be* at the bustling wharf at Schenectady. He and his father had come from the city by train. Between Schenectady and Albany, the canal descended steeply toward the Hudson River, with twenty-three locks close together. Passing through them took more than twenty hours. Travel-wise people avoided going through these locks by taking the train from Albany to Schenectady, cutting nearly a day from the trip between Buffalo and Albany.

Packets lined up every morning at Schenectady to take on passengers. Fast-talking hawkers met the trains and collared passengers as they got off. Each hawker boasted that his boat was the fastest, served the finest meals, and had the most comfortable sleeping accommodations.

The hustler who grabbed the lapels of Dennis's father's coat had shouted, "No packet's faster to Buffalo than the *Empire State*. She's the prettiest, fastest, most luxurious boat on the canal."

But his father had pushed him aside. "Away with you, man. We're for the *Glory Be*."

Once on board, Dennis had learned that most of the comfort the hawkers bragged about didn't exist. When darkness fell his first night aboard, he had been given a canvas hammock in the cabin. The cabin was divided by a heavy curtain. Women slept in the forward part, men in the aft. The hammocks were put away during the day, and the cabin was used for eating and sitting.

Hung three deep over each other, the hammocks hadn't allowed much room for the occupants. Dennis had been trying to make himself comfortable in his when a fat man climbed a small ladder and got into the hammock over him. Dennis had lain very still, afraid to take a deep breath, as the hammock sagged to within an inch of his chest.

During the night, the fat man had shifted continually, seeking a comfortable position. Each time he moved, the hammock sank a little lower, until it rested on Dennis.

Dennis had finally given up. He had squeezed out of his hammock and gone to the deck, where he rolled up in his blanket and leaned against the cabin to sleep.

Now, at O'Dowd's, Dennis was listening to the horns sounding up and down the canal. The voices of the freighter crews drifted over the water as the boats moved slowly along the canal.

When a passenger packet came up behind a slow freighter, the packet captain blasted his horn. The freighter was supposed to pull close to the towpath to allow the faster boat to pass. As the packet's horses passed the slow animals of the freighter, her towlines were raised over the heads of the freighter crewmen.

Freighter captains didn't like being passed and often were slow to move over. Shouting matches and a lot of horn blowing took place. If the freighter still didn't move over, a fight often broke out between the crews. To passengers, the fights were part of the entertainment on their trip.

As Dennis watched, a packet overtook a freighter in front of O'Dowd's. He began to draw the scene, his pencil flying across the paper.

Timmy, finished with his chores, came in from the garden. He stopped in the kitchen to give Kate the carrots, then went out to see what Dennis was doing.

Dennis looked up, but didn't speak.

"You're workin' hard, I see," Timmy said.

Dennis glared at him. "You," he said slowly, "talk too much."

Kate came through the door just in time. "Wash your hands," she said. "Both of you. Supper's almost ready."

CHAPTER
6

Patrick O'Dowd came for the boys after dinner the next day. "We'll take a ride along the canal," he said. "I expect Dennis would like to see it."

He rode Shannon while the two boys were on Tralee. "She's gentle," Timmy told Dennis. "Even you can ride 'er."

They rode west on the towpath toward Lockport. Boats passed traveling in both directions, and the boys waved at the crewmen and passengers.

O'Dowd suddenly reined Shannon in and said, "Listen!"

Timmy heard splashing water.

"Muskrats!" he said, pointing. A short way up the canal, three furry brown muskrats were playing tag in the water.

"Darned pesky critters," his father said.

As they rode closer, the muskrats paused to listen. Hearing their steps, all three animals made quick, expert dives and disappeared.

"Drat them!" O'Dowd said. "They've tunneled under the towpath."

"Is that bad?" asked Dennis.

"Muskrats like to tunnel into the berms," Timmy told him. "They dig until the berm is like a honeycomb. Then the tunnels collapse, and the berm sags and breaks open. They do it all the time."

Dennis said, almost to himself, "Muskrats. *Ondatra zibethica*. Fast-swimming water rat. Lives in swamps and rivers. Builds a nest chamber with an underwater entrance. Called a muskrat because of its strong smell."

Timmy looked at him suspiciously. "What did you say?"

Dennis laughed. "I read a lot and that's what I remember about muskrats. *Ondatra zibethica* is their Latin name."

"That come from books?" Timmy asked.

"Yes," Dennis replied. "Of course, I never saw one before. But I learned about them."

Timmy faced front again. "You ain't read much about shovels, that's for sure."

"Now wait a minute," Dennis began, but his uncle broke in.

"Timmy," he said, "mark the spot, and we'll get the pathmaster to take care of it tomorrow."

"This is old Mr. Storm's farm," Timmy said.

O'Dowd explained to Dennis. "The pathmaster'll poke into the berm to break the tunnels. Then he'll run patches of hay and brush down in it. The critters'll go back to their swamp, a mile or so back there, for a while. But they'll be back. They like to swim in the canal."

A horn sounded, and Timmy looked up and saw the *Glory Be* coming east. "It's Cap'n Sam," he said. "Back from Buffalo."

Billy, the hoggee, was whipping the horses into a lather. O'Dowd frowned. "Just what those muskrat tunnels need is waves from a speedin' boat! Why does that fool always have to play at record breakin'?"

The *Glory Be*, her blunt prow pushing wide waves across the canal, sped toward them.

O'Dowd glared at Billy as the team passed. He laid the end of his staff on the moving towrope. The rope carried the staff forward, and he watched its movement with an expert eye.

"He's doin' eight miles an hour if he's doin' an inch."

Cap'n Sam, at the tiller, watched the staff, and so did Timmy—in terror.

The *Glory Be* drew abreast of them. O'Dowd flagged Cap'n Sam down.

"Da! You ain't goin' to fine him!" Timmy cried.

"He's goin' too fast," his father replied.

"But . . ."

"Now, Timmy, speedin' is speedin'. I can't excuse Cap'n Sam, or others'll try to get away with it. Especially with the muskrats at work."

"But next summer, he said . . ."

O'Dowd shouted, "Sam, pull over."

The captain replied, "No need, Patrick. Just hop aboard. I'll give you the fine. Don't want to stop. We're tryin' for the Buffalo-to-Albany record."

O'Dowd stepped aboard the packet and held out his hand. Cap'n Sam laid a ten-dollar gold piece in it.

O'Dowd took the money. "Now tell your boy to slow those horses, or I'll fine you again."

Anger clouded Cap'n Sam's face. "I told you I'm atryin' to break the record," he shouted. "I'll pay your fines, but I'm not slowin' down."

"What you're doin' is breakin' down my berms," O'Dowd said.

The captain stared at him. The quiet swish of water passing against the hull was the only sound that could be heard. The passengers watched and listened expectantly.

The silence held for a full minute. Then O'Dowd said firmly, "Sam, slow this boat down or I'll have you barred from the canal."

Cap'n Sam glared, and O'Dowd glared right back. They faced each other like fighting cocks ready for a bout. The air tingled with tension.

Finally, Cap'n Sam gave way. "Billy," he yelled gruffly, "slow 'em down." He blew a protesting blast on his horn.

"Thank you, Captain," O'Dowd said, and stepped to the towpath. The *Glory Be* continued down the canal, slowing as she went.

Timmy, near tears, said, "I'll never 'prentice on the *Glory Be* now."

His father stared straight ahead as they rode on again. "Timmy," he said, "right is right, and rules are rules. I can't let Sam break the rules just so you can be his apprentice next year."

Timmy was so close to crying that he couldn't trust himself to answer. Then Dennis, behind him on Tralee, laughed. The sound drove Timmy to action. He rammed his elbow back as hard as he could into Dennis's ribs. The blow surprised his cousin and knocked him back over Tralee's rump. He tumbled to the towpath.

Timmy started to dismount. Dennis had already scrambled to his feet and was ready for him.

At the noise, O'Dowd turned in his saddle.

"Get back on that horse, Timothy," he ordered. His tone left little doubt about what would happen if Timmy didn't obey instantly.

Seething, Timmy did as he was told. Dennis remained

uncertainly in the middle of the towpath. O'Dowd said, "You, too, Dennis."

"Why doesn't he go home where he belongs?" Timmy grumbled.

"He belongs here," his father said, "and don't forget it again, unless you want a meetin' in the wash house."

Next morning, the sky sagged over the countryside like a gray awning. Thunder rumbled and rolled in the distance, and spikes of lightning poked down like probing fingers along the horizon. The heavy air was filled with foreboding. Birds had stopped singing and twittered nervously. In the stable the horses stomped anxiously.

Timmy and Dennis worked together in silence. When the horses had been curried, Timmy went off to get wood for the stove. Dennis sat on the porch, trying to draw. After a bit, he put his paper and pencils away and brought out a book to read.

The storm swept in just after dinner. The rain came hard and steady, whipped by powerful gusts from the west. Timmy prowled the keeping room, looking for something to do. Dennis sat with a book, ignoring the storm.

Grandfather brought checkers and a board from the bunkhouse.

"We're havin' a tournament," he announced. "Me against you two." He placed the checkers on their squares. "Loser gets to draw water from the well fer a week," he said, "and I never lose."

CHAPTER 7

Timmy heard the peddler's bells before anyone else at O'Dowd's. The tall, canvas-covered wagon was groaning through the thick mire of the dirt road behind the house. The bells on either side of the driver's seat clattered and jangled in an uneven rhythm.

The peddler, a heavily bearded man whose face was nearly concealed by a wide-brimmed black hat, shouted and clucked at his struggling gray horse, urging him to pull harder. A steady stream of water poured from the brim of his hat down the oilskin cape draped around his shoulders.

By the time the exhausted horse made the turn from the road to O'Dowd's, Timmy was at the door.

"Mr. Hayes is here," he yelled.

Kate said, "Oh, good. I can get that cloth I wanted." She went to a jar on a shelf over the stove and emptied a small pile of coins onto the table.

She said to Dennis, "This is my bank. I keep the money from my pies in it."

"Who's Mr. Hayes?" Dennis asked.

Kate counted the coins before answering. "The dry-goods peddler. He sells cloth by the yard, and I buy what I need to make my dresses and shirts for the men and the like. He travels up and down the canal in summer. It's a blessing to have him, so I don't have to go to town."

Kate wrapped the coins in a handkerchief, threw a shawl over her head to keep the rain off, and went to the door. "You ought to come see his wagon, Dennis."

The wagon stopped in front of the stable. Mr. Hayes's deep voice said, "Hello, Timmy. Your ma home today?"

"She's comin', Mr. Hayes." He laid his hand on the wet and winded horse. "He's all lathered. I better wipe him down."

"Now that'd be a fine thing to do, Timmy. Ned will thank you." He peered toward the stable. "Say, if you'd open them doors, I could drive him into the stable, out of the weather. That'd help a mite."

Timmy swung the big stable doors open, and the peddler tugged at the reins. Ned pricked up his ears and moved the wagon into the shelter.

Mr. Hayes climbed down. "These roads ain't much fun fer Ned on rainy days."

Kate came through the door. "Afternoon, Mr. Hayes. Not very pleasant, is it?"

Mr. Hayes looked at the sky piously and said, "Wal, ma'am, the Good Lord sees we git the rain we need. I guess we shouldn't complain 'bout that."

Kate smiled. "The Good Lord also knows that canawlers have trouble when there's too much rain, Mr. Hayes. I'd like it better if He remembered that, on days like this."

"Oh, true, ma'am. It ain't too easy on us peddlers, either. But it'd be worse if'n He held back on the rain. A drought is a sorry thing for everyone, dusty and all."

He opened the back door of his wagon and swept off his hat. "Won't you step in, ma'am, and see what nice goods I have today."

"Thank you, Mr. Hayes," Kate said, climbing the step

43

into the wagon. Dennis followed her inside. Both walls of the wagon were lined with bolts of fabric, hung on rollers so the material could easily be pulled off, measured, and cut for the customer.

Outside, Timmy wiped Ned down with a rough towel. "Easy, boy," he said in a soothing voice. "You can rest now." The horse turned his head and made a deep thank-you noise in his throat. The other horses watched with interest.

Timmy went to the back of the wagon. Kate was pulling out each fabric to judge the weight and color. Heavy bolts of calico and gingham prints hung on one side; white cotton sheeting, percales, and rolls of woolen suit cloth were on the other. She spent most of her time with the prints.

Mr. Hayes, beside Timmy, lighted a lantern and stuck his head in the door to hand it to Kate. "On a dark day like this, Miz O'Dowd, you can't hardly see the pretties. You'd best use this lantern."

Kate took the light and studied the fabrics she favored. Timmy watched Dennis, who had gone to the front of the wagon and was fingering a large bolt of white material.

Dennis turned to Mr. Hayes, "How much is this?" he asked.

"Nice canvas," Mr. Hayes said. "You've a good eye for cloth, lad. Fine material. Very popular."

"How much?" Dennis asked.

"Waaal," Mr. Hayes drawled, "considerin' it's so hard to come by, I'd say it's a bargain."

Timmy snickered. Mr. Hayes was a tough higgler and haggler. Dennis would lose this match if he planned to buy the material.

Kate said, "Come now, Mr. Hayes. You're stalling the boy."

The peddler cleared his throat. "Wal, I'd have to git seven cents the yard fer it."

Dennis exhaled. "That's expensive."

"Now, laddie," Mr. Hayes said, "you have to pay fer quality, and that's a real quality piece of cloth. 'Sides, things are only 'spensive when you don't git your money's worth."

Dennis felt the weight of the fabric.

He's tryin' to look like an expert, Timmy thought, and he really don't know nothin'.

"It's about right for oils," Dennis said. "I could stretch it on a frame and do a portrait of my grandfather."

Mr. Hayes was puzzled. "Oils? What's them?"

"Paints," Dennis replied.

"You gonna paint on that there canvas?"

"He's an artist, Mr. Hayes," Kate explained. "He draws and paints pictures."

"Oh," Mr. Hayes said. "Well, tell me, laddie. Just how much would you need?"

"A yard would be fine," Dennis said. "But seven cents"

Mr. Hayes stroked the raindrops from his beard. "Seein' as yer a new customer," he said, "might be I could give you a bit of a discount. You know, a special price. Say, six cents for the yard."

"Done!" said Dennis. "I'll get the money." He went past Kate to the back of the wagon, jumped down, and ran through the rain toward the house.

Timmy watched him splash across the stable yard. He's got his own money! he thought. He's showin' off again.

Kate found the materials she wanted and told Mr. Hayes how much she needed of each. While the peddler measured and cut, she looked out. The rain lashed across the yard in heavy waves.

"'Tis a terrible day, Mr. Hayes. I doubt your wagon can go very far on the muddy road."

"Oh, true, ma'am. Ned was just 'bout wore out when we got here."

"The captains have been telling us that the storm is all the way out into Lake Erie," she continued. "Like as not, we'll have rain for two or three more days."

Mr. Hayes folded the cloth he had cut from the bolts. Timmy saw him look inquisitively at Kate.

She turned. "I was thinking, Mr. Hayes, that I'm having a fine supper for the men tonight. And dinner tomorrow will be a good lamb stew."

Mr. Hayes waited expectantly.

"With the weather and all, 'twould be fine if you stayed for supper. You could sleep in the bunkhouse tonight. There's room."

She looked at him, and waited.

Mr. Hayes hemmed and hawed a little. "Ma'am, it's right nice of you to invite me. It truly is. And lamb stew tomorrow sounds dee-licious."

He paused, and Kate continued to wait.

Timmy smiled. He had seen his mother dicker with peddlers before. She had her own ways of making bargains.

Mr. Hayes cleared his throat again. "Aw, ma'am, I can't charge you the reg'lar price fer your goods if'n yer goin' to make me a guest and all."

"That's exactly what I was thinking, Mr. Hayes," she said. "As a guest, what would you want to charge me, do you think?"

The peddler pulled on his beard, raised his eyes to the wagon roof, and muttered to himself. Finally he said, "Might be I could take off what I'd pay fer a bed at the tavern. Would that be fair?"

Kate thought for a moment. "Yes, I think so. The price of the bed—and the price of two meals. I think that would be fine, Mr. Hayes. How much will that come to?"

"*And* two meals?" the peddler said. "Wal, I don't know . . ."

"My good lamb stew," Kate reminded him.

"Done!" said Mr. Hayes.

While he was figuring the bill, Kate turned to her son. "Unhitch Ned, Timmy," she told him. "Mr. Hayes is staying the night."

CHAPTER 8

The wet wind put an uncomfortable chill in the air. As Kate prepared supper, however, the heat from the big wood stove eased the dampness. Though it was only midafternoon, Timmy, Dennis, Grandfather, and Mr. Hayes had gathered in the keeping room, seeking refuge from the gloom outside.

Mr. Hayes and Grandfather talked about the old days on the canal. Mr. Hayes admitted that he was one of those who had been against the canal in the beginning.

"I said Clinton was daft with canal fever," he said. "I voted agin' him when he ran for gov'nor."

"Sure and I can see how you might do that," Grandfather said. "D'you feel different now?"

"By jeepers, yes," the peddler said. "The canal's the best thing to happen to New York since I was born."

Timmy lay on the floor, fingering his collection of arrowheads. He kept them in a small wooden box. Most had turned up when they plowed the hayfields, but he had traded neighboring boys for others and had found some on the canal berms. His favorite was a big chipped-stone point that Grandfather said was a spearhead. "Too big and heavy fer an arrow," he had guessed. "Probably a Mohawk."

The O'Dowds lived west of true Mohawk country, but Timmy knew the Mohawks had ranged as far as Lake Erie in their wars with other tribes. All the old settlers hereabouts had Indian stories to tell.

"This was real Indian country 'fore the canal came through," his father had told him.

Dennis had his nose in a book again. *All he ever does is read and draw*, Timmy thought.

Kate was slicing newly picked strawberries. "The last of the season," she said aloud, "but there may be enough for a shortcake."

Timmy looked up eagerly. "For tonight?"

"Maybe, if you whip me some cream," she said. "Can't have strawberry shortcake without whipped cream."

Timmy's mouth watered. "I'll whip you a whole bucket," he said with enthusiasm. "Maybe even more."

"Do it just before supper," she said. "It's too early now."

The front door opened, and Patrick O'Dowd came in, followed by an extraordinarily tall, thin man. The visitor ducked to avoid bumping his head on the door frame. Both men were wrapped in oilskins, which dripped on the floor. Before O'Dowd could close the door, a wet wind whistled into the keeping room.

Kate shivered. "Patrick, I'll thank you to leave the weather outside." Then she nodded to the tall man. "Well, howdy, Obediah. What brings you here today?"

Obediah Winter's voice was surprisingly big and deep, more like the voice of a barge captain than of the scarecrow he resembled.

"Howdy, Miz O'Dowd. I was walkin' my path when the super here came along. He allowed as how I might come in and dry out a bit." Winter removed his oilskin and hung it on a peg behind the door. On his back, under the oilskin, he wore a pack of straw. "More than just a mite damp out there," he added as he removed the pack and hung it next to the oilskin.

"Thought he might enjoy a bit of supper, Kate," Timmy's father said. "'Tisn't fit for man or beast out there. A little supper might keep Obediah alive, and I need him."

"We're going to have a full table, Obediah," Kate said, "but you're welcome if you don't mind taking what we've got."

Obediah's long, thin face brightened. "Ma'am, I've shared your table many times. Even your leavings would pleasure me considerable."

"Mr. Hayes is supping with us, too, Patrick," Kate said, nodding toward the peddler. "I couldn't let him drive old Ned through all that mud on a day like this."

O'Dowd glanced at the peddler, who was sitting with Grandfather. "Well, Mr. Hayes!" he said amiably. "I take it you sold Kate enough goods to wrap a camp of canal diggers and maybe leave some for a Sunday shirt for me?"

Mr. Hayes boomed from behind his black beard, "Aye, I did. But at a right fair price, I'd say. Wouldn't you, Miz O'Dowd?"

Kate laughed. "When you throw in the bed and board, Mr. Hayes, I'd say you got the best of the bargain."

Dennis slid across the floor close to Timmy. "Who's that?" he whispered. "He looks like Ichabod Crane."

"The pathmaster," Timmy whispered back. "Ichabod who?"

"You ought to read more," Dennis said. "Ichabod Crane is a character in a book by Washington Irving."

Timmy knew he had been stung again. He recalled that Mr. Worth, the schoolmaster, had books by Washington Irving and had offered them to him. Timmy hadn't taken the teacher up on the offer.

Without his rain gear, Obediah Winter seemed even taller and thinner than he had first appeared.

Kate nodded toward Dennis. "Obediah, this is our nephew from New York City, Dennis O'Dowd. You can sit for a spell and tell him about the canal while I brew up a pot of good hot Irish tea."

Dennis jumped to his feet, and Winter stuck out a long, thin hand. "Well, howdy, Dennis," he said. "This weather'll give you a poor opinion of our canal. Mostly, it's a beautiful thing to see."

"Yes, sir," Dennis said. "I know."

Winter, seeing the drawings on the floor, leaned over like a skinny pine tree bending in the wind. "Saaay, these pictures are right purty."

"Dennis is an artist," Kate said with a touch of pride.

The jealousy bug woke up and chewed at Timmy once more. *What am I?* he thought. *Nothin' but a stableboy, I guess.*

O'Dowd hadn't taken his oilskin off. "The berm is soft in a lot of places," he said. "I'm goin' to check the boat and supplies 'fore supper. Take your ease for a while, Obediah."

The pathmaster took a chair near Timmy and Dennis as O'Dowd went out.

"What does a pathmaster do?" Dennis asked.

Stretching his long legs before him, Winter sighed. "Walk," he said. "I been walkin' since sunup. Settin' feels good."

"He's the fastest pathmaster on the canal," Timmy threw in.

"Got the longest legs," Winter replied. Then he turned to Dennis. "Well, laddie, I walk the towpaths all the livelong day. You know, of course, that Mr. O'Dowd is the super?"

Dennis nodded.

"Well, I work fer him. There's half a dozen of us pathmasters that walk his towpath sections. We do whatever needs doin'. You saw my straw pack? That's what I use to patch the soft spots I see."

"I thought the hurry-up boat fixed holes," Dennis said.

"Oh, it does," Winter replied. "Big breaks. I patch the small uns and hope they don't get to be big uns. When a little break turns into a real breach, I run for the hurry-up crew. 'Sides that, I'm kinda the police man of my part of the canal. I stop crews from fightin' . . ." He looked at Grandfather. "That is, I stop 'em 'fore they gets too bloody. Too many fights to stop 'em all. I ain't brawny enough to do that, anyway. And I listen to the bellyachin' farmers. There's always one who thinks his bridge needs fixin' or somethin'."

"He fines the packets for speeding, too," Timmy added.

Winter laughed. "If'n I don't fine 'em, I end up patchin' the berms they wash away."

"Oh," Timmy said, "did Da tell you about the muskrats up at Storm's place? Looks like they've tunneled into the berm."

"Aye, he did, Timothy. I went and took a look. It ain't good. I busted the tunnels and laid in some patches, but, with this rain and all, that place could have trouble."

"What do you hear about the storm?" Mr. Hayes asked.

"The crews say we prob'ly got another day or two of it," Winter replied.

Kate brought the teapot. "Timmy, get the cups for me," she said. "Supper'll be ready in half an hour, so you better get to whipping the cream."

Timmy brought the cups. As he headed out to the cellar, where the milk and cream kept cool, he heard his mother say, "You going out again after supper, Obediah?"

"I have to, ma'am," the pathmaster replied somberly. "Got to keep a good eye on the soft spots in this weather. There's a couple of them could go any time."

CHAPTER 9

After supper, Timmy's father went to the big desk on the far side of the keeping room. He took a roll of canal drawings from a shelf, spread the sheets on the desk, and turned up the lantern to full brightness.

Timmy looked at the drawings with him as his father marked spots on the canal he had noticed were especially soft. Older marks on the drawings indicated where breaches had burst through the berms at earlier times.

Finally O'Dowd sighed and rolled up the drawings. "No way I can tell what's goin' to go next, Timmy," he said. "But we've got to get the water level down another foot."

He put on his slicker. "Saddle up Shannon for me, son. I'm goin' to ride to the lock, to see that the sluices are open and drainin' as much water as possible."

"'Tis a poor night for ridin', Patrick," Grandfather told him.

O'Dowd shrugged. "What would you have me do, Da? I can't just sit here in comfort and wait for somethin' to happen."

"I could ride along with you," Grandfather suggested. "The company might be good for you."

"Not on your life, Da. But I'm grateful to you for the thought." He turned to his wife. "I'll be back by mornin'," he said. "Obediah is walkin' up the canal. He'll run back if need be, and Sean can get the crew out."

O'Dowd came back while they were at breakfast. His face, drawn with fatigue, was grim. The rain continued to sweep down the canal.

Kate fixed his place at the table. "You need some food, Patrick. Sit."

Timmy was just finishing his oatmeal. "Is the water level goin' down?" he asked.

"Sluices are drainin' as fast as they can," his father told him, "but they're just stayin' even with the rain. We can't get the level any lower. The canal's full to the brim for a hundred miles."

When he had eaten, Kate said, "Get some sleep, Patrick. You'll need it later."

After breakfast, Timmy watched the rain from the porch. The canal water lapped near the top of the berms. A few tow teams splashed by, sloshing through puddles on the towpath.

Dennis stood next to him. "Sure aren't many boats out today," he observed.

"All the captains smell trouble," Timmy told him. "They're tied up, waitin' to see what'll happen."

Just before noon, the sky began to lighten. After a final burst, the rain slackened, and the wind died down. Grandfather and Mr. Hayes came over from the bunkhouse.

"It's lettin' up," Grandfather said.

Mr. Hayes peered at the sky and sniffed the air with an

expert nose. "It'll be over in an hour, Michael. Look at the sky to the west."

Low on the western horizon, a bright band of sky seemed to be pushing upward against the dark clouds.

"Thank you, Lord," Grandfather said fervently. "It's just in time."

Timmy looked at the high water in the canal. "I hope so, Daideo. But it'll take a couple of days for the water to go down. We aren't through with it yet."

A wistful look came into Grandfather's eyes. "It rains all the time in County Mayo," he said. "But not like this. It's soft rain, the kind that makes Erin so green. And there're always rainbows, 'cause the sun is never far behind the rain."

Dennis looked at his grandfather. "Would you like to go back?" he asked.

Grandfather put his hand on Dennis's shoulder. "No, boy-o, I wouldn't. Oh, I still love the old sod, but a man can't put rainbows on the dinner table. The canal's the place fer me now."

He paused, then said, "Y'know, me and Donal and Patrick are all lookin' for one thing—a future fer you and Timmy. Yer the next in the line of O'Dowds."

He eased himself into a chair. "New York State's the place fer you. You can go to school here, and you can have what we never had. That's why yer father's so set on school fer you, Timmy. He's better off than I was, and he wants even more fer you."

"There's someone runnin' on the towpath," Mr. Hayes said. "See him?"

Timmy saw the running figure coming toward them. After a moment, he said, "That's Obediah—gallopin' like a ghost was after him!"

Winter's long, skinny legs enabled him to take tremendous strides, and he covered the distance quickly. His oilskin streamed out behind him, and he appeared to be shouting.

As he ran onto the wharf, his voice reached them, but it was another minute before they could make out his words.

"She's breached!" he was shouting. "She's breached at Storm's place."

He was gasping so hard that he had to struggle to get the words out. "Where's the super? She's breached, and it's a bad un."

"The muskrats!" Timmy cried.

"Worst I've ever seen," the pathmaster panted. "Whole wall's cavin' in."

Timmy's father appeared in the doorway, rubbing his eyes to break through the curtain of sleep.

"When, Obediah?" he asked.

"Started an hour ago. Old man Storm was out, tryin' to help with the patchin', but it warn't no use."

O'Dowd, now wide awake, took command. "Da, roust out the crew and get 'em goin'," he ordered. "Timmy, saddle Tralee and ride to the farmers. Tell 'em we need help. We'll pay regular wages. Take men, women—anyone willin' to work. Hire all the teams of oxen you can get. We'll pay for them, too. Dennis, ride the hurry-up boat. You can hand out tools."

He was already getting into the oilskin that Kate had handed him. "Hayes, get to the wharf and warn the captains. Tell the eastbounders to get to the lock fast as they can. Warn the westbounders there's a bad break ahead."

Kate said, "I'll get the pots. The men'll be needing coffee and soup."

CHAPTER 10

Timmy, wrapped in an oilskin, rode west along the muddy road, guiding Tralee to the edge, where the footing was fairly sure. The mare picked her way carefully, trotting faster when the ground was solid under her. The rain no longer pelted them, and that made the ride easier.

He knew most of the families at the dozen or so farms along the road. Boys from the farms went to the one-room school with him in the winter. The first place belonged to fat Mr. Mueller, who was standing in the stable doorway as Timmy rode in.

Mueller squinted to see who it was. He didn't recognize Timmy at first.

"Canal's breached!" Timmy shouted as Tralee pulled up.

Mueller caught a glimpse of Timmy's face. "That you, young O'Dowd?"

"Yes, sir," Timmy said, looking down on him from Tralee's back. "The berm's breached bad at Storm's place. We need help. Can you and the boys come?"

Mueller slowly poked a hoe handle into the mud in front of the stable and contemplated the question. "Bad day fer it," he said. "Got work of our own."

Timmy had rounded up farm help before. He knew what to expect. Each farmer wanted to know about the pay. Cash was always short on farms, and chances to earn it were always welcome. But these men were a careful, cagey lot.

He said, "Da's payin' full wages. But you gotta be quick or it'll be too late."

Mueller's interest picked up but he didn't move. "Full wages, you say. In cash?"

"Yes, sir," Timmy said. "Paid at the boat, soon as the job's done."

"I got three boys."

"I know 'em. We'll pay them, too."

"All of 'em?"

"Full wages," Timmy replied. "But you gotta move now."

Mueller wasn't quite ready to move. "My wife can outwork all of us."

"She's hired," Timmy said.

Mueller warmed to the conversation. "Wal now, that's five of us. How about oxen? You need my team?"

Timmy had almost forgotten about the teams they'd need to haul trees to the breach. "We'll take them," he said. He swung Tralee around. "Get there as quick as you can!"

"Wait a minute, young'un. We ain't finished yet. What're you payin' for my team?"

"Six bits for the day," Timmy said, remembering what he had heard his father offer other times.

Mueller brightened. "Wal, that's fair. But how do I know you're authorized? How do I know you ain't trickin' me."

"Jehoshaphat, Mr. Mueller!" Timmy cried in frustration. "You know my da! What would he do if I played tricks about the canal?"

Mueller laughed. "Ya! Oh, ya! He's a fast man with a birch rod. All right, young'un, you got a deal."

Timmy left Mueller's and urged Tralee to gallop as they rode from farm to farm. But no matter how he pushed, the recruiting was slow. Every farmer haggled over the wages.

He almost lost some. At the Martin farm, beefy-faced Mrs. Martin took charge of the conversation from the start, while Mr. Martin stood by, silently staring at the ground. She bargained and bargained. How much? How long? Were they supplying meals? What if the work went on all night? Timmy thought her questions would never end.

She showed no sign of agreement.

Her next question was, "How do I know we'll get paid? I only got your word."

Timmy's tension peaked. He snapped, "I guess we don't need you after all," and started out of the yard.

"Don't get snippety with me, boy," she called after him.

"I'm not," Timmy said over his shoulder, "but if we talk much longer, the canal'll be dry."

Mr. Martin finally spoke up. "Martha, go into the house. The canawlers allus paid before and they'll pay now." To Timmy he said, "I'll be there."

Only old Schlessinger refused to listen. "Ach, let the dummed water run out," he said, "and good riddance. Ditch never should have been dug in the first place."

Timmy tried to argue. Schlessinger picked up a shovel and waved it menacingly. "Off'n my property," he yelled. "I don't want yer money!"

Timmy rode Tralee out of Schlessinger's barnyard quickly. The last words he heard were, "And don't come back!"

When he had hired all the men and teams he could find in the area, Timmy turned Tralee toward Storm's place.

CHAPTER 11

As he rode up, Timmy saw the great gaping wound where the towpath should have been. It looked as though a hungry giant had taken a twenty-five-foot bite out of the canal berm. Torrents of water tumbled through the break into the farm fields beyond the berm. Mr. Storm's farm was already a lake.

The break was the biggest he had ever seen—maybe too big to plug. The berm, he knew from his father's drawings, was twelve feet wide at the towpath and thirty-six feet wide at the base. None of it was left! Every bit had been washed out. The water roaring through the break ate hungrily at the remaining berm. Every few minutes, new sections collapsed, and the break widened.

If they don't plug it soon, Timmy thought, *the whole berm will go.*

The water level of the canal had already dropped. That morning, it had lapped at the edge of the towpath. Now it was down half a foot. The boats needed three feet of water to float, but they wouldn't have it much longer.

Timmy glanced at the sky. The clouds had cleared, but the sun was already low in the sky. Darkness would come along before the crews could finish the repair.

He saw that his father had fanned crews out into the

nearby woods to search for trees. The thunk-thunk-thunk of their axes echoed down the canal, mixing with the shouts of the men and the roar of rushing water.

He rode to the break. Men up to their chests in water battled the angry deluge pouring from the canal. They drove three-inch log pilings into the bottom of the breach. Two men slipped and struggled in the current to hold a log upright while two others swung heavy wooden mallets to drive it down into the soft bottom.

These pilings, spaced ten feet apart, were to anchor tree trunks, which would be floated into the break later. The trunks, lodged across the break, would slow the racing water and serve as the backbone of the new berm.

He swung off Tralee near where his father stood on the towpath. O'Dowd, eyes bright, surveyed the damage and barked commands through a speaking trumpet. On the hurry-up boat, tied near the break, Dennis was handing out tools as the men came to him.

Sean Connarty pulled himself out of the water and climbed to the towpath.

"It's bad," he said, wiping water from his face.

O'Dowd lowered his speaking trumpet. "Worst I've seen. Can we stop it?"

Connarty shrugged. "Mebbe. And mebbe not."

Two freight barges pulled in near the hurry-up boat. The crewmen ran over.

"Can you use us?" one called.

"Gladly," O'Dowd shouted. "Get axes at the boat there. Work with the cuttin' gangs."

"If this ain't stopped soon," one yelled, "we'll be settin' in mud for a month."

O'Dowd nodded and turned to Timmy. "Good job of turnin' out the farmers."

"I got all I could."

O'Dowd spotted a crew of boys, girls, and farm wives pulling tree branches and brush toward the break.

"Haul those over here!" he bellowed. To Timmy, he said, "See that they stack that up for bonfires. We'll need light after the sun goes down."

Timmy quickly selected places on the path for the fires. "Put it here, and here," he yelled at the brush haulers.

When half a dozen fires were burning brightly, Timmy ran to the hurry-up boat.

He waved to his mother, who had set up a makeshift kitchen on a high hump of ground near the towpath. She and half a dozen women were making coffee and soup in big kettles hanging on spits over a fire. They passed hot mugs to the exhausted crewmen who staggered out of the water.

Dennis watched the men in the break.

"Never seen anythin' like this in New York, I bet," Timmy said.

"No," Dennis agreed. He pointed to the crews in the woods on either side of Storm's farm. "What're they going to do with those trees?"

"Watch," Timmy answered.

As soon as the axmen felled a tree, a dozen men hacked away the branches. When the trunk was stripped clean, a team of oxen, leaning powerful shoulders into the work, dragged the log through the muck to the towpath.

As the boys looked on, the first log was rolled into the canal with a splash, and the turbulent water quickly swept it toward the break. As it gained speed in the current, the log bucked, tumbled, and twisted. The men in the water grappled with it and finally wrestled it into the break.

They swung it across the breach, with its ends lodged against the standing berm sections. The rushing water pushed it firmly against the pilings.

"See, that's the way the logs mend the break," Timmy told Dennis.

"But logs won't stop the water. It'll go right around them."

"At first it will," Timmy said. "But when more logs are in there, the water'll slow down. Then we'll dump in brush to slow it even more."

Connarty was out of the water again. He sipped a mug of hot coffee as he and O'Dowd conferred near the hurry-up boat.

"Can we get those logs in place soon enough?" O'Dowd asked.

"I dunno," Connarty answered. "That berm is breakin' pretty fast. The breach's growing quicker'n we can fill it."

O'Dowd studied the break. "There's no point in puttin' brush in there until those logs are solid."

"And we can't make 'em solid as long as the berm keeps collapsin'," Connarty said. "The pilings alone aren't enough."

"There's got to be some way to slow that water," O'Dowd said. "Got any ideas?"

Timmy and Dennis exchanged ominous glances.

Dennis frowned. "You ever read about the British navy, Timmy?"

Timmy stared at him. "What's the British navy got to do with us?"

"In sea battles, cannonballs rip holes in the hulls of ships. The crews have to repair the holes at sea or the ships will sink."

"You read too much," Timmy said.

"Listen," Dennis said. "They repair those holes with canvas. The ships always carry extra sails, and they cover the holes with them."

"Good for them," Timmy said. "So what?"

"You're not listening! They run sheets of canvas down the outside of the hull across the holes. Then crewmen dive in and nail the canvas in place. That stops enough water so they can stay afloat."

Pictures flashed in Timmy's mind as suddenly he saw what Dennis was trying to tell him. "You mean we could run canvas across the logs to slow the water?"

"Why not? That'll stop the water faster than brush or anything else," Dennis said.

Timmy turned toward the men struggling in the breach. It might work, if only they had a big-enough sheet of canvas.

"Forget it," he said. "Where are we goin' to get that much canvas?"

Dennis was excited. "Mr. Hayes!" he shouted. "He has a whole big bolt of it!"

Timmy's father, hearing the shout, turned around. "What's this about Hayes?" he demanded.

Dennis explained how the British navy used canvas in repairs. O'Dowd and Connarty listened.

Connarty looked at the breach. "Could work."

"But has he got enough of the stuff?" O'Dowd asked.

"A whole new bolt," Dennis said, "lacking the yard I bought. It's more than a yard wide and maybe sixty feet long."

O'Dowd considered the break for a moment, then turned to Connarty. "Sean, run the hurry-up boat back and get that canvas. Move, man! Sooner you get there, sooner you'll be back."

CHAPTER 12

Hayes sat protectively on his bolt of white canvas, the brim of his hat flapping in the wind, manning the tiller with one hand as the hurry-up boat raced up the canal. Sean Connarty, astride Mayo, reined the horses to a stop near the break in the berm.

Shouting to be heard over the din, O'Dowd was giving instructions to six men gathered on the berm. As the boat bumped against the towpath next to him, he said, "Here's that canvas. Let's go to work."

Hayes looked up without moving from his cloth. "You buyin' this bolt?" he asked suspiciously.

"Every inch of it," O'Dowd assured him.

"Eight cents a yard," Hayes said.

Timmy protested. "You told Dennis it was seven cents!"

"This is different," Hayes replied.

"Different how?" Timmy asked.

"He's buyin' my entire stock. I won't have none left to sell."

"He should get it for less. He's buyin' the whole thing. You won't *have* to sell any more," Timmy said.

"Stop it!" O'Dowd ordered. "The berm is cavin' in fast. Make it nine cents and quit the arguin'. Get that stuff up here!"

Hayes jumped up. "Nine it is!"

The crewmen leaped into the hurry-up boat and hoisted the heavy bolt to the towpath.

"Get hammers," O'Dowd told Timmy and Dennis, "and a keg of nails." He turned to the workmen. "Slide the bolt into the water at this end of the break. Unroll it across the face of the logs, and nail it as you go."

Connarty dropped into the canal to guide the bolt of canvas as the other men lowered it. He nailed the end of the cloth to the top log in the break. The other men hopped in behind him, holding the bolt against the logs. The dry canvas wanted to float. The racing water pulled and sucked it away from the logs.

O'Dowd saw this. "Quick! Nail it to the logs as you unroll it, or it'll get away from you," he directed. "Unroll a foot at a time. Put a nail in every log."

It took two men to unroll the canvas in the swirling water. Two more followed as nailers and drove nails into the top and bottom logs. Two more followed them, completely securing the canvas. The water whipping around them slowed the work, but they eased the material across the break foot by foot.

Timmy and Dennis watched from the hurry-up boat. About six feet of the canvas had been nailed down when Timmy shouted, "It's workin'! It's stoppin' the water."

O'Dowd lifted his speaking trumpet again. "Brush haulers," he boomed, "get brush and branches over here quick."

He turned to waiting crewmen on the berm. "Start feedin' brush down in front of the canvas. Lay it on thick!"

By the time the canvas had been stretched halfway across the breach, what was happening was clear. Behind the newly nailed canvas, the water barely trickled between the logs into the field. On the uncanvased side, water still poured through. The farmers not working in the break ran over to watch. They cheered as the canvas was nailed.

It was now dark. The flickering light from the bonfires glistened on the wet faces of the men in the water.

O'Dowd roared into his speaking trumpet, "Enough sightseein'! Everyone turn to! Get brush and branches over here now. We can finish this up if you bend your backs into it.

"Miller, Storm, Schmidt," he called, "bring shovels and barrows from the boat. We'll need dirt from the field soon as the brush is in."

Within the hour, the canvas was in place. The entire crew carried brush to the canal and stuffed it into the water in front of the logs. In a short time, the new berm took shape. The farmers, seeing the work about finished, began to bring their tools back to Timmy and Dennis at the hurry-up boat. O'Dowd paid each worker from a sack of coins.

Hayes was sitting on the hurry-up boat as the boys put the tools back on their racks.

"That was a right smart idea, laddie," he said to Dennis. "You ought to be a canal engineer. You could teach a few things to some I've met."

"He read it in a book," Timmy said.

Hayes wagged his head. "Wal, you can't beat books fer learnin'. Wish I had more schoolin'. I only barely can write and cipher. You lads have the chance to do better."

"Timmy's going to be a canal engineer," Dennis told him. "He's going to college."

"I'm goin' to be a packet captain!" Timmy insisted.

"I've always wanted to be the captain of a packet, like Cap'n Sam."

Hayes tugged at his beard. "Don't take me wrong, Timmy," he said. "Captains are fine people. But mostly they dress like dandies, and holler and blow their horns. When you come to think about it, that ain't much. Kind of a lot of fuss and feathers and not much brainwork."

"Cap'n Sam runs a fine boat!" Timmy protested. But down inside, he felt funny. What Hayes said made sense: a lot of fuss and feathers.

The moon had set and the night was black by the time Timmy's father took Kate and the boys back to the house. The temporary berm was in place and holding. During the week, the hurry-up crew would go back and finish rebuilding the towpath.

Grandfather was waiting for them, snoozing in his rocking chair, chin resting on his chest. He wouldn't go to bed until he knew they were safely back from the breach.

Timmy and Dennis, with eyes already half shut and feet dragging, climbed to the loft. They undressed and slid into their beds with little more than a goodnight grunt to each other.

As he drifted off to sleep, Timmy remembered his father standing straight and commanding on the towpath. He could hear his strong voice issuing orders through the speaking trumpet. He was proud of the way the farmers had listened and followed his orders.

Patrick O'Dowd didn't have a tall hat or a fancy coat, but he didn't need them. People respected both him and his knowledge of the canal.

Then, quite suddenly his vision changed. The man on

the berm wasn't his father, but was himself, and he seemed to be in charge. He stood tall on the path, directing the repair crew through the speaking trumpet. They all looked up at him with respect, and listened when he gave orders.

The warm glow that settled over him carried him deeper into sleep.

CHAPTER 13

Timmy awoke to see that Dennis's bed was empty. He dressed and hurried down the ladder.

"Dinner's almost ready," Kate said.

"Dinner?"

"You slept most of the morning."

Timmy shook his head to clear the cobwebs. "Where's Dennis?" he asked. Good smells from the big stove floated through the room, reminding his stomach that it had missed a meal. He went over to the stove to look. "What's for dinner?"

Kate laughed. "To answer one question at a time, Dennis is out front with Grandfather, and fried chicken."

He lifted the cover of his mother's big skillet and peeked in. Golden pieces of chicken were turning a lovely crispy brown. She had just finished mashing potatoes to go with the chicken and was piling a fluffy mound in a serving dish. The sight and the aroma were exquisite torture.

"How long?" he asked.

Kate turned and hugged him. "Can you wait five minutes?" Then she said softly, "I was proud of you yesterday. You did a fine job."

Timmy snuggled against her. "The canvas was Dennis's idea," he said. "It was good, wasn't it?"

"I'm proud of him, too. The two of you are a pair of real O'Dowds." She kissed the top of his head. "Now scoot out there and get Grandfather and Dennis for dinner."

"Where's Da?" Timmy asked as he started for the door.

"He and the crew are at Storm's, working on the berm. They won't be back for dinner. I want you to take a basket of fried chicken to them as soon as you finish eating."

Outside, Grandfather was sitting on the porch so that the sun fell on his face. Dennis, with a pencil in his hand, faced him. The canvas he had bought from Mr. Hayes was tacked to a wooden frame and propped on a tall chair in front of him.

Dennis smiled. "Hello, Timmy. You awake?"

"No. I'm walkin' in my sleep," Timmy replied tartly.

"Sorry I asked," Dennis said.

Timmy saw hurt dart through Dennis's eyes and instantly wished he had said something else. "Aw, I guess I'm just hungry." He nodded at the canvas. "Whatcha doin'?"

"He's paintin' me picture," Grandfather said, obviously pleased.

Timmy examined the canvas. Dennis had sketched an outline in light pencil lines. Even though the lines were rough, the picture already looked a lot like Grandfather.

"You're not paintin'. You're drawin' in pencil," Timmy said.

"That's the sketch. After dinner, I'll begin painting." He deftly added a few more lines. "This is going to be in oils," he said. "I sketch first, then I paint. I've been learning to use oil paints, but I never did a whole portrait before."

Grandfather's nose lifted. He sniffed the air and stood up. "I smell fried chicken."

"Oh, I forgot," Timmy said. "Dinner's ready."

"Well, let's get at it! Not even me picture is likely to keep me from fried chicken."

Dennis collected his art materials.

Timmy started into the house, then turned back to his cousin. "I'm takin' fried chicken to Da and the crew after dinner. Want to come?"

Dennis's answer was a big smile. Then he looked at Grandfather. "But I was going to start painting."

"Whoosht, boy!" Grandfather said. "Go along with him. I'll be takin' a small nap anyway. We can paint when you get back."

Riding back from Storm's, Dennis said, "The hurry-up crew sure likes Uncle Patrick a lot."

"It's 'cause he's smart and knows what he's doin'."

"They look up to him," Dennis said.

They rode in silence for a couple of minutes. Then Timmy said, "They know he could do most anything he put his mind to, I 'spect."

"You ever think about being a section superintendent like him?" Dennis asked.

Timmy shook his head. "Da says that once the canal is rebuilt, the super's job will be different. They won't need hurry-up boats any more."

"That why he wants you to be a canal engineer?"

"I guess so," Timmy said. He recalled the picture of his father standing on the towpath the previous day, giving orders through the speaking trumpet.

"You know, a canal engineer would be in charge of buildin' a whole canal. He'd boss hundreds of men. And he'd know all about buildin' locks, and makin' tight berms, and all that."

"Like Uncle Patrick last night?" Dennis asked.

Timmy nodded. "Only more."

Timmy watched Dennis prepare his oil paints. He poured powder from a small box into linseed oil, then worked the mixture with a small stick.

"You make your own paint?" he asked.

"Right," Dennis said. "These powders are colored pigments. I mix each with the oil to make batches of primary colors, like red and blue, and also black and white. Then I blend those to make the shades I need."

He dipped a brush in the red paint he had just mixed and dabbed some on his palette. He dipped the brush again, this time in white, and worked it into the red on the palette. The red turned to pink. He touched a tiny bit of brown into the spot, and then a dab of yellow.

"That's going to be the flesh color," he said.

"Can I watch you paint?"

Dennis shook his head. "Sorry. You can't see the picture 'til it's finished."

"Why not?" Timmy asked, instantly miffed.

"Because that's the way artists work."

Timmy started to protest, then thought better of it.

Grandfather, settling into his rocker, said, "Let him get on with his work, Timmy. He won't be here much longer."

The next morning, as they left the stable after their chores, Dennis said, "I'm going to miss the horses."

"I thought you didn't like the stable."

"I got used to it."

Timmy grinned. "You got used to shovelin' manure?"

"I said I'd miss the horses, not the manure," Dennis replied, making a face. "Especially Tralee. She likes me."

Timmy looked at him. "You ought to stay here longer. It'd do you good."

"A couple more weeks with you and they'd never let me back into New York City."

They moved amiably toward the house. Dennis said, "I might even ride on your boat when you're a captain."

"You can decorate the cabin," Timmy said. "You could make it really grand. Hand-painted pictures! That'd be even better than the *Glory Be.*"

Later in the week, Cap'n Sam was back with the *Glory Be.* He nosed the packet in to the O'Dowd wharf. This time Kate was ready for his passengers, with plenty of apple pies.

While the passengers ate their pie slices, Timmy went down to the boat. Cap'n Sam was chatting with a passenger. Timmy waited until the passenger turned away, then said, "Cap'n Sam, about next summer . . ."

The captain stared at him. "Well, what about it?"

"Well, about my da . . ."

Blunt looked puzzled, then suddenly understood. "Oh, you mean about the fine he slapped on me, Timmy. He was just doin' his job." He fished a big watch from his vest pocket. "Gettin' late," he muttered, and shouted, "All aboard, ladies and gentlemen. Time to move along."

The passengers were already on their way back to the packet. "You ready, Billy?" Cap'n Sam called.

Then he again took notice of Timmy, standing near the tiller, looking forlorn.

"You know I deserved the fine, don't you?" he asked.

Timmy nodded.

The captain looked at him. "Timmy, your father is the most honest straightshooter I know. A lot of men would wink at my speedin' if their boy was goin' to work on my boat. But not your father. No, sirree. Not him."

Timmy felt his stomach tighten.

Cap'n Sam reached over and grasped his shoulder. "You know what a man of principle is, boy?" he asked.

Timmy shook his head.

"It's a man who's true to his word and what he believes in, no matter what. That's your father, Timmy. He's a man of principle."

Timmy didn't know what to say. Was the captain telling him he could be his apprentice next year or not?

"I think some of that could rub off on you, Timmy," Cap'n Sam concluded. "That's why I want you with me on the *Glory Be* next year."

Cap'n Sam was saying yes. Timmy kicked into the air and let out a whoop. The packet had already started to move up the canal. He leaped to the wharf.

"Oh," Cap'n Sam called after him, "tell your grandfather I'll pick up your cousin next Tuesday."

That night after supper, Timmy tugged at his father's sleeve as they left the table.

"Da, can I talk to you? Private-like?"

His father said, "Come down to the wharf while I check the hurry-up boat. We need to replace a lot of supplies."

On the boat, O'Dowd said, "What's on your mind, Timmy?"

Timmy picked up a length of loose rope and began to wind it around his hand and elbow to make a coil.

"It's about next summer," he said. "Cap'n Sam says he wants me to 'prentice with him."

His father nodded. "And . . .?"

"Will you let me go for the summer?"

O'Dowd sat down on a nail keg. "You can make more of yourself than a barge captain, Timmy."

"I've been thinkin' about that," Timmy said. "I'm not sure I want to be a captain any more."

Timmy felt his father watching him.

"What changed your mind?"

Timmy shrugged. "Oh, I don't know. Maybe it was workin' on the breach last night. I'm not sure."

"So you don't want to go aboard the *Glory Be* next summer?"

"Yes and no," Timmy said. "It's hard to decide. Until last night, I wanted to very much. Now . . . well, now I'm not sure."

The two sat quietly for a while. The last streaks from the setting sun fanned out across the western sky, then slowly faded.

Finally, his father said, "I've an idea for you."

Timmy looked at him.

"You go on the *Glory Be* next summer. You'll learn a lot about the canal—the whole canal, not just our section here. And you can leave your wages with me. I'll put 'em in your college fund."

"You mean you want me to be a packet captain?"

"No. I just think workin' a summer on a packet could teach you a lot. Might help when you study engineering. We'll tell Sam you're going to work for him for a summer or two only."

Timmy thought about this. He had dreamed so long about being a packet captain. Now things seemed to be changing. He still wanted to be a captain, but not as much. He found himself comparing his father to Cap'n Sam. Somehow the captain didn't seem as impressive or as important any more.

"I think I'll like Rensselaer," Timmy said.

On the way back to the house, his father spoke again. "After a summer on the *Glory Be*, you'll know better what you want."

"It'll be college," Timmy said, now feeling positive about it. Suddenly he was relieved. The decision had weighed on him for a long time, and it felt good to have made it.

"Next summer," he said, "I could take a week off the boat and visit Dennis in the city."

"Good idea," his father replied.

CHAPTER 14

"The *Glory Be* will be here in a little while," Timmy's mother said, handing Dennis a hamper. "I've packed a few things you like—a pie, a loaf of bread, and some of my homemade grape jelly. You can eat them on the boat."

Dennis took the hamper and thanked her. He and Timmy had already carried his carpetbag and his canvas case down to the wharf.

"All right, macaroni," Timmy said. "You're makin' a big mystery of Grandfather's picture. You goin' to show it to us or not?"

"Sure am," Dennis said.

By now, the men of the hurry-up crew, Timmy's mother and father, and Grandfather had all gathered in front of the house. The painting, still propped on the tall porch chair, was under a flap of cloth. All through the past week, Dennis had kept the cloth in place when he wasn't working on the picture. No one had been allowed to see it.

Now Dennis stepped up to the painting. With a flourish, he pulled the cloth away.

Everyone crowded close.

After examining the picture for a minute, Timmy said, "It even looks like him—sort of."

"What do you mean, sort of?" Dennis demanded. "Could you do better?"

Timmy laughed and shook his head. "I still say you paint better than you shovel." He stepped closer to examine the detail in the picture.

Grandfather was posed sitting in his rocking chair on the porch. Timmy's eyes searched the background Dennis had painted—the tall grass behind the house. Suddenly he saw a tiny face, topped by a little green hat, peeking out between weeds. Timmy blinked and looked twice to make sure his eyes weren't playing tricks.

"The leprechaun!" he said. "You put the leprechaun in the picture!"

"Sure enough." Kate laughed. "That fool leprechaun got himself into the picture."

Timmy protested. "Macaroni, you know there's no such thing as a leprechaun!"

Dennis's eyes twinkled a little, like Grandfather's, and he shrugged.

"An artist can paint only what he sees," he said.

From far up the canal came the faint sound of Cap'n Sam's horn.

THE ERIE CANAL—THEN AND NOW

The Erie Canal, built between 1817 and 1825, was an impossible dream that came true. Constructed by daring men who had little idea of how to build a canal, it proved to be the engineering marvel of its time.

Getting ready for the project, the canal company advertised across the country for canal engineers to design and supervise the work—but no one answered the ads. There wasn't one such engineer in the entire United States at the time.

The planning went ahead in spite of this, using men who were available—mostly land surveyors. One of these, Canvass White, was sent to England, where he walked two thousand miles beside the British canals, sketching locks, aqueducts, and towpaths. His drawings were the only instruction manual the Erie builders ever had.

What the canal builders *did* have, however, was native "Yankee" ingenuity. When they ran into a problem, they scratched their heads and figured out a solution. No one could tell them the right way to do anything, so they invented new ways for themselves.

The Erie Canal has been called the first great American school of engineering, because the builders taught themselves as they worked.

The canal diggers had only picks, shovels, and muscle

to move an enormous amount of dirt from the ditch, and to build earthen walls on each side of it. To make the task more difficult, the canal cut through heavy forests. Trees and underbrush had to be cleared before a shovelful of dirt could be turned.

In the first days, axmen cleared only three or four trees a day, because it took so long to remove the big stumps. The diggers had to wait for tree crews to get the stumps out before getting on with their own work. Newspapers poked fun at the project, saying that the canal might be finished in forty years—if it didn't rain too much.

Then the head scratching began. Someone devised a huge stump puller, with eighteen-foot wheels supporting a strong winch. After a tree was felled, the stump puller moved in. Its chains were tied around the stump, and the winch turned. In a few minutes, even the toughest old stump popped from the ground. Crews cleared forty or more trees a day with the stump puller, and the digging went a lot faster.

In most places, networks of tree and bush roots criss-crossed the soil. A man might spend hours cutting through tough, sinewy roots—and not move much dirt.

Again, inventiveness saved the day. Most canal men had been farmers, and they understood plowing. One invented a new plow, with an extra set of very sharp blades. The plowing blades made the earth easy to work; the cutting blades chopped the roots to bits. This left only loose dirt for the diggers to shovel into wheelbarrows.

Wheelbarrows, too, were a canal invention. At first, dirt was carried in small carts. Then someone realized that dumping dirt would be faster than shoveling it from a cart, so the one-wheel wheelbarrow, to be dumped in an instant by the man who pushed it, was invented.

The original canal was a 363-mile ribbon of water with

eighty-three locks. It spanned New York State from Buffalo, at Lake Erie, to Albany, on the Hudson River.

Initially, many politicians argued against the construction of the canal, saying it was impractical and too expensive. However, Governor DeWitt Clinton and a group of foresighted planners saw the great value of a route that would connect the cities of the east to the wilderness of the western United States, and they pushed ahead with the project.

Clinton's judgment was proved correct. In its first year, 13,000 boats and 40,000 westbound settlers used the new canal. Travel from Albany to Buffalo was shortened from six weeks to as little as six days.

The Erie Canal cost about $7 million to build—an enormous amount of money in those days. Yet it not only paid for itself in less than seven years, but also made money for the state of New York for many years. Freighters paid a toll according to the weight they carried. Passenger boats paid six cents a mile.

Canal traffic produced revenues so great that the New York legislature thought of canceling all real estate taxes and using canal income to pay state bills. They didn't do it—but they thought about it.

A canal like the Erie is more than just a long ditch or a man-made river. The land it traverses is not level, and canals must have ways of lifting and lowering boats as the terrain requires. This lifting and lowering is done by locks.

A lock is like a big box with ends that open and close. A boat sails into a lock and that end is closed behind it; water flows into the lock to lift the boat; the other end of the box is opened, and the boat sails out, now ten or twelve feet higher than before entering the lock.

The Erie Canal required locks because Lake Erie is 571

feet higher than the Hudson River. Eighty-three locks were needed along the route of the Erie to lift and lower barges.

The Erie Canal had to cross eighteen rivers along its route. To accomplish this, the canal builders built eighteen great stone aqueducts—bridges that carried the flowing canal water over these rivers. For early New Yorkers, the sight of a "river crossing a river" was wonderful to behold.

After the Erie was built, the canal system was expanded. Additional canals were built to connect the Erie with Lake Champlain, with Oswego and the Thousand Islands area of the St. Lawrence River, and with New York's beautiful Finger Lakes.

Today, more than 140 years later, the Erie Canal still operates. It is now known as the New York Barge Canal, and is very different from the original.

During its lifetime, the canal was widened and deepened to accommodate larger barges. It was rerouted. New sections that shortened it by fifty miles were dug. The original eighty-three locks were replaced by fifty-seven larger, more efficient units.

The use of the canal changed, too. First railroads, then airplanes took the passenger traffic from the old Erie. Then freight began to move by rail and by truck. In time, the steady stream of freight barges dwindled.

Today, the canal is used chiefly by pleasure boats. More than 110,000 recreational boaters enjoy the scenic vistas along the canal routes each year. Eighteen hydroelectric plants in the system provide electricity for the surrounding country. The canal system supplies fresh water to many communities and water to farmers for irrigation.

The old Erie hasn't completely disappeared. Details of

life along the canal are preserved in a number of museums. A few of the old locks have been preserved just as they were at the height of canawling days. And you can still see the five great double locks at Lockport.

The Erie Canal, sometimes called the "Grand Canal," will always be remembered for the great contribution it made to the growth of this country.

GLOSSARY

Aqueduct: A stone bridge carrying the Erie Canal over a river. Eighteen aqueducts were used along the route of the canal. New Yorkers were fascinated by the sight of "a river crossing a river." The Rexford Aqueduct, crossing the Mohawk River, is still standing, a tribute to the fine quality of the masonry work performed by the Erie builders.

Berm: Any earthen embankment. Today, residential areas are sometimes screened from nearby highways by berms. Safety berms are constructed around oil-storage tanks to contain the oil in case of a leak or a fire. On the Erie Canal, the two banks were berms. The towpath was on one; the other was known as the heelpath.

Deep Cut, The: A channel cut through solid rock for nearly two miles just west of Lockport, New York. A million and a half yards of stone had to be blasted out and carried away to make it.

Feeder: A river or stream feeding water into the Erie Canal to maintain the proper water level.

Freighter: Canal boat that carried only freight, no passengers.

Heelpath: A name for the bank of the canal opposite the towpath.

Higgler: A peddler who went from house to house selling his wares. He "higgled and haggled" over prices with his customers.

Hoggee: A boy who drove the horses on the towpath. The boy was usually between fourteen and eighteen years old, and was paid $10 a month for his work—or about $70 for the months in which the canal was open. As a young man, President James A. Garfield was a hoggee.

Hurry-up boat: Small, fast boat that carried men and materials to patch big leaks in the canal walls.

Line barn: A barn in which a company operating on the canal kept horses and mules, so its boats could change teams frequently—usually every six hours.

Line boat: A boat carrying both freight and passengers. It charged a lower fare than the passenger packet, and was therefore popular with families moving their possessions to farms out west.

Lockmaster: The man who opened and closed the lock gates. He lived beside his lock, worked twenty-four hours a day, and was paid $25 a month plus room and board. He was also called the "locktender."

Lockport Five: The most famous locks on the Erie Canal, located at Lockport. They were five dual locks—for boats going in each direction. They lowered (or raised) boats a total of sixty feet down (or up) the rocky face of the Niagara Escarpment. No locks like them had been built anywhere before.

Macaroni: A dude, a dandy. Originally an English description of a fancy dresser, the term came to America during the Revolution, when soldiers of a Maryland regiment that wore fancy uniforms were called "macaronis." The word occurs in "Yankee Doodle":

> Yankee Doodle went to town
> A ridin' on a pony.
> Stuck a feather in his hat
> And called him macaroni.

Oilskins: Coats and hats made of cotton material waterproofed by treatment with oil and gums, usually worn by sailors. Also called "slickers."

Packet: On the Erie Canal, a barge that carried only passengers. Packets usually had the best food and sleeping accommodations available.

Pathmaster: A canal employee who walked sections of the canal daily. He made minor patches in the berm, assessed speeding fines, listened to complaints, and generally served as a policeman in his jurisdiction.

Sluice: Any channel controlled by a floodgate. On the Erie Canal, sluices were opened to drain excess water from the canal during heavy rains. This prevented overflowing of canal berms.

BIBLIOGRAPHY AND
RECOMMENDED READING LIST

CANAL STORIES

Adams, Samuel Hopkins. *Canal Town: A Novel*. New York: Random House, 1917.

— *Chingo Smith of the Erie Canal*. New York: Random House, 1953.

— *The Erie Canal*. New York: Random House, 1953.

— *Grandfather Stories*. New York: Random House, 1953.

Edmonds, Walter D. *Drums Along the Mohawk*. Boston: Little, Brown & Co., 1936.

— *Erie Water*. Boston: Little, Brown & Co., 1933.

— *Rome Haul*. Boston: Little, Brown & Co., 1929.

— *The Wedding Journey*. Boston: Little, Brown & Co., 1947.

HISTORY OF THE ERIE CANAL

Chalmers, Harvey, II. *How the Irish Built the Erie*. New York: Bookman Associates, 1964.

Condon, George E. *Stars in the Water: The Story of the Erie Canal*. Garden City, NY: Doubleday & Co., 1974.

Drago, Harry Sinclair. *Canal Days in America*. New York: Bramhall House, 1972.

Harlow, Alvin F. *Old Towpaths*. New York: D. Appleton & Co., 1926.

Meadowcroft, Enid LaMonte. *Along the Erie Towpath*. New York: Thomas Y. Crowell Co., 1940.

Payne, Robert. *The Canal Builders*. New York: The Macmillan Company, 1959.

Powell, Alexander E. *Gone Are the Days*. Boston: Little, Brown & Co., 1938.

Shank, William H. *Towpaths to Tugboats*. York, PA: The American Canal and Transportation Center, 1982.

Shaw, Ronald E. *Erie Water West*. Lexington, KY: The University of Kentucky Press, 1966.

Walker, Barbara K., and S. Warren. *The Erie Canal: Gateway to Empire*. Boston: D. C. Heath & Co., 1963.

Wibberley, Leonard Patrick O'Connor. *The Coming of the Green*. New York: Henry Holt & Co., 1958.

Wyld, Lionel D. *Low Bridge!: Folklore and the Erie Canal*. Syracuse, NY: Syracuse University Press, 1963.

Wyld, Lionel D., ed. *40' x 28' x 4': The Erie Canal—150 Years*. Rome, NY: Oneida County Erie Canal Commemoration Commission, 1967.